DEVASTATION

BY FLENARDO

BOOKS BY FLENARDO

THE POETIC WHORE

MARRIED TO THE PEN

FORBIDDEN FORGIVENESS

Copyrighted @2023 by Flenardo L. Taylor

All rights reserved, therefore no part of this book may be reproduced, distributed, or transmitted or by any means, including photocopying, recording or other electronic or mechanical methods without written permission of the publisher, except in the case of brief quotations embodied in critical reviews and certain other noncommercial uses permitted my copyright law.

Publisher's Note: This is a work of fiction. Names, characters, places and incidents are products of the author's imagination. Locale and public names are sometimes used for atmospheric purposes. Any resemblance to actual people, living or dead, or to businesses, companies, events or institutions are completely coincidental.

Published by
    Creolistic Ink Publishing
    Hahnville LA 70057

Edited by Marsha Dickson

Graphic Designed by Pbimbola (Fiverr)

ISBN: 9798394849619

Thank You

DEVASTATION

Chapter 1

Devin's phone rattles and illuminates on the nightstand.

He buries his face in the pillow as his fingertips continuously tap the touchscreen to turn off the alarm.

He retrieves his phone. "Five AM," he mumbles, placing the phone on the nightstand.

He slides out of bed, rolls out his yoga mat, and executes a child pose to begin his morning meditation.

After releasing negative energy from his body and mind, he performs various pushups and abs exercises. He flexes his chisel pecs and runs his hands over his tight eight-pack. "Sexy, single, and successful," he recites in the mirror.

He basks a few more seconds before walking inside the master bathroom. *Courtside* by *DVSN* plays through the Bluetooth radio.

He glides his briefs down his legs, flings them in the hamper, and dances his way to the shower.

There isn't a more satisfying feeling than closing out his morning regimen with a masturbation session.

FLENARDO

He forms a strong fist and squeezes his dick until a thick vein forms over the tatted word *Devastation*.

An old flame gave him that name, and he makes sure to speak life into his dick daily. He places his left forearm against the shower wall for support and gently slides his fist back and forth, circling the tip with his thumb and gliding his fist down. Eyes drift to his dick, "are you ready to cum this morning?"

He flaps his dick against his abdomen in a nodding response. Grabbing a handful of his locs, he yanks himself from the wall. He clenches his butt muscles and fucks the inside of his palm. The more hair he pulls, the harder he tugs on his dick.

Tears seep from his eyes and run down his cheek. "Damn, this feels so good," he grunts.

Stroking faster, his hand slips off his dick from the combination of water and precum mixing. He wraps his hand back around his dick again, closes his eyes and fantasizes about tunneling through some deep, sloppy pussy.

"Bitch, give me this pussy!" he screams. "What's my fucking name?"

His eyes expand, leaving wrinkles on his forehead as he returns to reality.

DEVASTATION

He grinds his teeth, fingernails sinking into his palms as he slides them over his dick. Cum explodes from the opening and plasters the shower wall like caulk.

He smiles wide and waves good-bye to his kids as they drip from the wall and down the drain.

He leans against the wall. "Whew, now my morning is complete."

He grabs the Africa Axe shower gel, sniffs the fragrances, and lathers his skin.

After rinsing and drying off his body, he steps inside his closet. He scratches his head and shifts his jaw from side to side as he decides on his attire for casual Friday.

He chooses a pair of jeans and a sweater and matches them with black calfskin Christian Louboutin boots.

He skips down the stairs, enters the kitchen, and opens the refrigerator. Shifting a few items over, he grabs a banana and cream protein shake, and drinks it as he exits the penthouse.

Car horns, local businesses, runners, and the sweet scent of pussy lingers as he walks down Washington Ave.

"Good morning," he greets and smiles at a blonde-hair, blue-eyed woman wearing a black crop top legging set.

She's sexy, but he's not interested due to his trust issues with his ex-girlfriend. She was his eternal flame, and her pussy tasted like God had dropped it from heaven.

He remembers the time he purchased a princess-cut center diamond ring from Tiffany & Co. He had rushed to her place from work with a smile, heart thumping, and unspeakable joy.

He recited his engagement proposal outside her apartment door. He inhaled and breathed out his last moment of nervousness before unlocking and opening the door.

The Tiffany bag slipped from his fingers and dropped to the floor.

He catches his girlfriend on her knees while some random stranger plunges his dick into her mouth repeatedly.

He balled his fists while charging and struck the stranger with a right hook.

Simone stands between the stranger and him. "Devin, stop! Please stop. I'm so sorry," she pleads.

"Cheating ass slut. I ought to kick your ass too. All the time I invested in our future, and I feel betrayed in the worst way."

DEVASTATION

Fighting back the tears and staring at his fiancé's naked and sweaty body, he snatched the Tiffany bag from the ground and vowed never to speak to her again.

"Watch where you are walking. You bumped into me and spilled my latte," she said,

"I apologize. Daydreaming caught the better of me. Can I buy you an-"

Before he could finish the sentence, she opened the lid and threw a cream-colored liquid all over his sweater.

"What's the fuck is your problem?"

She rolls her eyes. "Your zombie-walking ass should watch where you are going."

"My apology is sincere. I'd offer to buy another one but fuck you and your stank ass attitude."

"Fuck you with your fake Rastafari-looking ass."

He scrunches his face, exhaling to gain his composure. "I'm going to turn around because I'm not one to argue with a wanna-be hood rat white girl."

He turns around and retreats down the street as her cuss words chase behind him.

He removes his phone from his pants pocket and dials his boss. "Today is shitty. Please put me down for telework."

FLENARDO

DEVASTATION

Chapter 2

Jonathan detaches his mouth from Vee's pussy lips and wipes his mouth and chin. "What's the fuck! Are you trying to give me lockjaw? I've been down here for thirty minutes, and you haven't cum yet."

She rolls her eyes, bridges her hips, and shoves his head between her legs. "You talk too much. Just eat."

She closes her eyelids, rotates, and grinds his face with intense pleasure. "Now, your mouth has a purpose. Munch, crunch, and enjoy your lunch."

She presses and guides the back of his head deeper. "Aww yeah, I'm going to enjoy creaming on your face," she moans.

Squeezing her thighs against his head, she says, "you are going to drown in this pussy tonight. All that shit you were bragging about. You better pull apples out of me like you're inside the Garden of Eden."

He bites on her lips before sliding his tongue up and down while she squeezes the piercing on her nipples with her fingers.

"Damn, you are making me so wet. Keep sucking my clit," she moans.

He nosedives and swipes his tongue left, right, and faster than before.

I wish this jackrabbit would slow down and focus on one spot. I'm never going to cum, she thinks while faking her emotions.

She stops him and suggests, "maybe I'll cum quicker if you let me take control and smother my pussy over your face. Suck this pussy, boy. You know you like the way I dance on your face," she boasts.

She cups his dick in her hands and sinks her newly pedicured toenails into his nutsack. Droplets of blood run in the crest of her cuticles.

"Ohh, Ohh," he utters in pain. He pushes her face away, hoping that she will stop.

She ignores his request, expands her jaws, and sucks his balls to soothe his discomfort.

"Vee, your mouth is magical. Can I please have some head?"

She grips his dick tighter, bobs her head, and jerks his meat in her mouth.

She stops sucking his dick for a second and screams, "make me cum, Daddy!"

DEVASTATION

She returns to her deepthroating position.

He presses his hands over her ass cheeks and forces her to fuck his face harder.

Her saliva drips off the side of his dick and runs down his thigh. She trails her tongue to his mushroom tip, licks over his urinary meatus, and gobbles again.

He spreads her lips wider, jabbing his tongue forward and backward.

She jerks her fists faster around his dick, kissing the head every time it peeps through her hand.

"Oh, Oh, Oh, Oh, shit. Suck it!" he shrieks. Cum erupts and lands on the side of her cheek.

She slides her pussy away from his face, hops off the bed, and shuffles to the bathroom.

She opens the shower door and turns on the water to drown out Jonathan's sorry excuses from the bedroom.

"Vee, I'm sorry. Next time, I promise not to bust until you get yours," he guarantees.

She sits on the toilet, drops her head, and covers her ears.

"Vee, did you hear me?" he asks.

She walks to the doorway. "Don't worry, your brother eats and fucks better anyway!" she shouts. "Let yourself out, and don't come back."

"Damn, it's like that? Can a brother wash up first?"

She looks to the left, smiles, and throws a pack of baby wipes in his direction.

"You crazy bitch!" he yells.

"Fuck you! With your non pussy eating ass. Lock my door and send your brother next time."

She closes the bathroom door, grabs her vibrator, and fucks the frustration away.

After a mighty nut, she cleans her body and her dildo. She slips on an oversized T-shirt and writes tonight's episode in her diary.

Nympho Log: 15 March 2022

Unsatisfied with the male species name Jonathan, the non pussy eater. Side note: I'll make sure to fuck his brother in the future. To be honest, it wasn't his fault I didn't cum. My mind was on that sexy muthafucker I threw coffee on earlier today. I'm going to name him Chocolate Latte, and I'm going to suck his cream. Nympho out.

She closes her diary and powers on her iPad. Emails, coupons, bills, and fuck requests flood the screen while she searches for a novel to help her sleep.

She deletes them one by one and pauses when she sees an email from Ms. Shantae.

It's an invitation to reconnect with the group. It reads,

DEVASTATION

Good morning, Veronica,

I hope this email finds you in good spirits. It has been two years since you vowed never to return. I have prayed daily for you, especially for your safety. I'm not here to judge your lifestyle, but I need you to know I love and miss you.

Please come and listen to my special guest speaker if you are free next Friday. He is one of our founding members, and I believe he could impact your life.

My number is still the same.

You can reply yes to the email or call me if you are coming to the session.

See you soon.

Love, Ms. Shantae.

She misses the relationship advice from Ms. Shante, a former sex addict who didn't take any shit from anyone she was helping to recover.

Deep down, Vee wants transformation in her life. Hopefully, she can experience it before hitting rock bottom. Since the age of twenty-one, Vee has lived comfortably from the settlement she was awarded. She refuses to get a job and spends time chasing dicks, clits, and swingers' conventions.

Joe Joe, her Boxer, comes over, blinking his sad eyes, and places his head in her lap.

She agrees to come to the session, sends a response, and closes her iPad.

"Joe, are you ready to go outside?"

He springs up on all fours, wags his nub of a tail, and runs to the door with his tongue hanging out.

She slips on a housecoat and slippers and picks up his leash.

"Come on, Joe Joe. You can shit in Michael's yard. That will teach him to be truthful the next time someone asks if he has a girlfriend."

DEVASTATION

Chapter 3

After busting his ass through college and working low-level entry jobs, Devin has become the most sought-after software developer in St. Louis.

The company executive announces, "and employee of the year is… Devin William."

He rises from his seat, shoulders back, chest poked out, and chin high. He winks at his haters as he takes long strides to the stage. He shakes hands and smiles at the board before preparing his speech for his colleagues.

"Fourscore and seven years ago, our forefathers.…"

After quoting the first line of the Gettysburg Address, he pauses and watches the blank stares on the audience's faces.

He taps the mic with his palms, and the sound causes the audience's attention to return to the podium.

He turns away and bursts into laughter.

"I'm only playing, but on a serious note, gratitude and honor go to God for allowing me to fulfill my purpose and my team for always motivating me to push for more significant goals."

At work, he's always professional, but tonight everyone will know he's the fiercest software developer in the country.

He lifts his plaque over his head and yells, "who's ready to get shit-faced?" The atmosphere of the banquet transforms from business to a party once the Djay music vibrates the room.

The female bartender places individual shot glasses down the counters and mixes whiskey, rum, vodka, and orange juice for the first round.

Devin bows to the distinguished guests and leaps off the stage. He gulps the first shot down his throat. "Ahhh," waving his tongue at the bartender. "What do you call this?"

She continues shaking another round and answers, "Hot Damn."

He lifts two fingers in the air, signaling for a second round. "That's my type of drink. Keep 'em coming."

Devin grabs two drinks, finds a seat and watches his peers dance to *Twerkulator* by *City Girls*.

A female voice interrupts his watch party. "Is this seat taken?"

He shifts his gaze upon her, "Ms. Yu Yan, I believe you have the power to sit anywhere you choose.

Your parent chose the perfect name for you because you have the most radiant smile I have ever seen."

"I'm not easily impressed, but your compliment made me blush. Someone has been studying Chinese birth names on their off time."

He lifts his hand, squeezing his index finger and thumb almost together, "just a little bit."

He stands and wipes down the seat next to him with a napkin.

She takes a seat, crosses her long sexy legs, and continues to engage in their conversation.

"Devin, your loyalty and commitment to my company is a turn-on, and money saturates my panties. You are an arrogant bastard, but your passion and drive are immeasurable. How would you like an opportunity of a lifetime and oversee my company's production in Beijing?"

"Ms. Yu Yan- "

"Call me Diana," she interrupts.

"We're on a first-name basis now? Okay, Diana, I find your offer gratifying, and I'm sure the salary is twice as much."

He passes Ms. Yu-Yan a shot. "Let's toast to your proposal, and please allow me some time to consider it."

"One last question, Mr. Williams."

"Sure, ask away."

"Why is the company's most illustrious and delicious man afraid of relationships?"

He laughs momentarily before responding. "Work is a priority, and distraction is the devil's work. But the main reason is deceit. I will never trust a woman with my heart again."

"Once again, I can see why you are perfect for my company."

She looks down at his smooth hands. "Let me see your palms," she demands.

He flips them over as suggested, awaiting her following statement.

She runs her fingers along his marriage, heart, and heath lines. "It appears you haven't beaten the success off your hands. If you decide to work for me, I'll make sure to include weekly fuck funds for your pleasure."

"Fuck funds? Now you have my attention, Ms. Diana. The thought of you being on the menu has never crossed my mind."

"Calm down, young man. I'll never sleep with people who work for me. My fuck funds consist of beautiful and endless women to keep you stress-free.

DEVASTATION

"I'll never hire anyone without knowing their background. You have an intriguing extracurricular hobby."

His mouth falls over, and before he says anything embarrassing, he finishes his drinks and informs Ms. Diana he will be in touch.

She rubs his shoulders and responds, "huí tóu jiàn," which means see you later.

His eyes follow her to the executive table, where she connects with her other clients.

"What the hell happened? Background check on what I do with my dick and money. I need another fucking drink," he said.

He springs from his seat, snaps his fingers to the music, and dances to the bar.

"If you don't mind, can you strengthen the drinks?"

"No problem," she obliges.

The bartender slides his drinks toward him. "Here you go. It would be best if you sipped these cautiously," she warns.

He throws the first one down, slams the glass down, and does the same with the second one.

"Now that's a fucking drink!" he yells.

Devin spends the rest of the evening watching coworkers lose their minds over alcohol and pussy.

The team leader sneaks into the ladies' room to fuck his new intern, promising her a free ride up the corporate ladder. Of course, they always fall for his bullshit and end up shredding papers as his assistant.

His phone vibrates against his thigh, and a mischievous grin appears on his face. He retrieves his phone, and the message reads, *Daddy, this mouth isn't going to fuck itself.*

His dick jumps in his pants from the text message. He fists bump one of his coworkers. "Enjoy yourself; I'm going to slide out," he hints.

He tips the bartender, says farewell to his friends, hugs Ms. Yu Yan, and calls an Uber before walking out the door.

The driver's location is minutes away, and he can't wait to face fuck Thirsty. She has the type of pussy that makes you dehydrated all day until you can taste her.

He recalls the one time he refused to drink water. His friends found him passed out under his desk. They revived him, and he swore he was exhausted from work.

"Are you Mr. Devin?" an 80's looking nerd inside a Honda Accord asks.

"Yes, I am." His mind was somewhere else.

He slides in the seat, closes the door, and rides to the peaceful suburbs of Clayton.

His dick pulsates through his pants from thinking about their last fuck session.

The Uber driver pulls to the curb before he can place the car in park. Devin jumps out and runs towards her doorstep.

He fumbles with the keys until he steps in and finds her in a velvet trim thong set sitting on her knees.

She crawls to him, unzips his pants, and pulls out his dick.

She smiles while massaging his dick. "Daddy, are the kids ready to come home?"

She slaps his dick across her left cheek and trails it over her nose before shoving it in her mouth.

"Hell yeah, they are ready to come down your nasty throat."

He lifts his arms, removes his shirt, and tosses it on the floor. He grips his fingers around her chin. "Look at me," he demands. "I won't be here long," he said.

He thrusts his dick forward, backward, and faster while she gags. Pulling his dick out of her mouth briefly, she tongue-licked his balls.

While stroking his dick, she moans, "fuck my throat deeper."

He kicks off his shoes, loosens, and unbuckles his pants. Everything falls to the floor, and he stands in black socks with a hard cock.

He leans in and wraps both hands around her head. She opens her mouth and bobs nonstop, swallowing his inches without breathing.

He vigorously plunges her throat until he is ready to cum. His load is thick, but she knows she doesn't get paid unless she drinks it all.

He presses down on her head and fucks her mouth.

"Ooh shit, Thirsty," he grunts.

His booty cheeks tremble, his eyes twitch, and he yells like a banshee.

"Ahh. Ahh. Ahh."

He cums in her mouth, and she continues sucking until he can't take it anymore.

He pushes her away. "Damn, Thirsty. Stop trying to swallow my soul."

"Baby, I can't help it. Your cum tastes like milk and honey. I wish you would fuck the shit out of me tonight," she proposes.

DEVASTATION

Her phone chimes, notifying the Cash App payment he sent.

"Maybe I will. Perhaps I won't. But one thing is for certain, you will always get paid for fucking with me."

FLENARDO

DEVASTATION

Chapter 4

Vee's heart thumps hard in her chest, and her hands constantly tremble. She has bitten two nails, anticipating tonight's session with her old friends.

"What am I going to wear tonight?" she ponders as she slides the hangers over in search of an outfit. She skips the seductive look and chooses an olive fleece jogger with a matching hoodie.

The jogger outfit reminds her of the time she saw the guy's dick print sitting next to her, and hopefully, he will be in attendance.

The soothing thought sends tingles through her nipples. She squeezes them tightly and clears her mind before she is enticed to finger fuck her pussy before leaving home.

She fans her hands in front of her panties, "Calm down, girl. Mommy will find you a face to ride."

She applies makeup, slips on her clothes, ties her hair in a bun, and strolls out the front door.

She notices Michael, her next-door neighbor, washing his car. She walks past him without saying a word. He throws the rag in a bucket and sparks a conversation.

"Vee, please give me a minute to explain."

His cologne lingers through her nostril, and she tries to ignore his voice instead of looking into his beautiful green eyes.

Please don't give in, she thinks to herself.

She takes a breath and expresses her feelings.

"Michael, I thought you were different. I shared my life story with you. If you only wanted some ass, you could have been upfront instead of acting like a cowering bitch. I deserve dick without drama. We could have been perfect fuck neighbors, but noooo. You ruined that shit. Speaking of shit, Joe Joe will fertilize your yard every morning and hopefully twice at night."

"Vee, you are childish."

"Childish? You haven't seen anything yet. Wait until I tell your girlfriend about your ass-eating fetishes."

She pushes him in the chest, "get the hell out of my way before you make me late to my meeting."

She walks away with a satisfied smile after resisting temptation and telling a man how she feels about being fucked over.

She honks her car horn, and Michael turns around. She flips him the middle finger and reverses out of the driveway.

DEVASTATION

She rides to the meeting, singing her favorite songs until she reaches CityPlace Center, a professional facility overlooking a three-acre lake with a fitness trail.

She remembers the first time she came to class and told Ms. Shantae, "this place is too beautiful for whores."

Ms. Shantae hugged her and asked, "were you expecting a drug-infested halfway house?"

She chuckles from the past joke and finds a new song to sing as she walks to the door. She enters the building, waves to the security guard, and waits for the elevator to take her to the meeting.

The doors open to her floor, and her eyes scan the vibrant and colorful artwork hanging on the wall. Once she approaches Ms. Shantae's door, she feels numb and has second thoughts.

"Come on, Vee, you can do this," she mumbles.

The thing that motivates her is sex, and she knows she is wrong for thinking about the one thing that is killing her mind and soul.

She closes her eyes and imagines sucking a hard precum leaking dick. Her pussy moistens from the fantasy of swallowing nuts while the class cheers, "eat that dick."

She feels someone brush against her shoulders.

"Are you going in or going to stand outside like you have a dick in your ass?" the mysterious woman asks.

The woman grabs Vee's hands and pulls her through the door. "Let's go, hoe," she commands.

Vee entered the rooms but could not locate Ms. Shantae. She sits in the rear of the conference room and remains quiet.

The mystery woman writes on the whiteboard, 'Art of selling and buying pussy.'

Today's topic puzzles the group, and one brave man raises his hands. "Who are you, and where's Ms. Shantae?"

"Who am I?" she responds. "I Am that I Am."

She pulls out a black twelve-inch lifelike suction cup dildo and slams it on the table. She slaps the dildo, and it waves side to side like a tree blowing in the wind.

"I'm not here to answer your questions. I'm here to make money off the backs of you muthafuckers."

A female gathers her belongings and walks toward the door. The mystery woman yanks the dildo off the table and catapults it in the air, connecting it to the back of the female's head.

"Sit your cum-laden ass down somewhere," she demands. "Now, back to my statement, and don't ask me shit else," she reiterates.

"My name is Asperilla Valdez, and I'm your new sex teacher. Rule number one for you bitches; stop crying when your dumbass fucks a man, and he never calls you back. We are going to drain his balls and his pockets. To the gentlemen buying pussy, you will spend more because the quality of pussy in St. Louis is about to become more valuable than Bitcoins. Excuse me, sir. Why are you typing on a laptop during my campaign speech?"

He lifts his head from the screen and smiles.

Asperilla's eyebrows rise higher after seeing an old client. "Devin? Oh my God, I had no idea you were in St. Louis."

Vee zooms her attention on the front row and realizes it was the guy she threw coffee on last week.

She finds him fascinating and curious about why he's in the class. She turns her head in another direction, avoids eye contact, and slides down in her seat.

The doors to the conference room open, and Ms. Shantae enters the class with a handsome and stylish gentleman.

He grips Asperilla by the wrist. "What the hell are you doing?"

"I'm in the middle of teaching. There's money to be made off these hoes."

He points to the rear of the room, "have a seat. I'll deal with you later."

Asperilla claps her heels together and spins around. "Yes, Daddy," she answers.

Ms. Shantae erases Asperilla's topic and informs the class about her special guest.

"Good afternoon. It's a pleasure to see you all this evening. You are about to witness redemption in the flesh. The guy standing next to me was my first client, and I asked him to come and share some encouraging words. I present to some and introduce the one and only Malakai Valdez to others."

The group stands and claps as Malakai approaches the front of the room.

"It's my honor to be here, and tonight will be the first step in regaining your power." He walks toward the door, picks up the dildo, and throws it in the trash. "There's a time to fuck and never a time to be fuck over," he quotes.

Chapter 5

Malakai pulls his arm through his sleeves, removes his coat, and places it on the back of the chair.

He stands in front of the room and claps his hands together. "Can I have your attention? I won't degrade or make you feel unworthy because you like to fuck. Being a whore in rehab takes discipline. You will do some stupid shit along your journey, but you can and will conquer your sex demons.

"I have been in St. Louis for two months and can expose details about everyone in this class. You all need to do better when it comes to your surroundings and your sexual excursion. If you're not willing to change, I encourage you all to invest in life insurance because chasing dicks, tits, pussy, and ass will send you to an early grave."

He looks in Vee's direction; "Excuse me. Who's your sponsor?"

"I don't need one."

"Sure, you do; everyone needs someone who knows the feeling of waking up with a cum-over. I will create a lifeline for you and the rest of the class.

"Devin, stop hiding behind that laptop and connect with the class. I believe you and Ms. 'I don't need anyone' could be perfect for each other," Malakai suggests.

Devin turns around to the back of the room, and his face cringes at the sight of seeing Vee.

"Malakai, I trust your judgment, but please find anyone except that lunatic," he pleads.

"Are you sure you aren't attracted to her?" Malakai asked.

"Hell no! I wouldn't let her suck my dick with Kylie Jenner's lips."

"Watch your mouth, Mr. Williams," Ms. Shantae advises.

Malakai walks over and pats Devin on the back. "Congratulations. I'm synching you with your lifeline partner right now."

Malakai leaves Vee and Devin confused as he walks around, pairing members for their new adventure.

Once he links everyone, he opens the class for discussions and questions.

DEVASTATION

"Did Asperilla influences you to change?" a young female asks.

"Yeah. Changed continents so I could escape all the chaos she causes," he jokes. "On a serious note, she plays a loving role with our beautiful daughter and me. They are the rock and soul of my life.

"I had to change to protect them because my past actions resulted in a close friend's death. I don't expect you all to change overnight. We are whores in rehab for a reason, but I promise, after this assignment, you all will become more conscious of your decisions."

Malakai returns to the podium and recites a poem.

What is your pussy worth,
and who deserves your stroke?
So why give it away freely
without thinking of the consequences?
Dicks. Side chicks.
People become pussy whipped
from the taste of another man or woman's lips.
The word says,
'Do not cast your pearls to swine
or give what is sacred to dogs
because they will turn,
trample them under their feet,

and tear them to pieces.'

He becomes silent and allows the room to analyze his poetic words.

"Ms. Shantae, you are welcome to have your class back. I'll return in a year to see which partners have improved lifestyles," he announces.

He interlaces his fingers with Asperilla and walks out the door without looking back or saying a word.

"Class, under your chair is an envelope. Please reach down and open it," Ms. Shantae instructs.

The class was ready to open the envelope and find the details, but Asperilla returned to the session and retrieved her dildo from the trash can.

"I'm not leaving my dildo in the trash for you hoes to slobber over," she said.

She hugs Ms. Shantae and leaves the room.

Vee lifts her hand in the air. "Is she serious about making us sell pussy?" she asks.

Ms. Shantae responds, "she'll probably have you fucking a donkey in Mexico."

When the class noticed she wasn't smiling, they decided not to mention Asperilla's name anymore.

"Let's discuss this envelope. You all have rules to follow, and I will give homework assignments to help you with your goals. Please be safe and text your partner when you arrive home. Class dismissed."

Vee was the last to leave her seat. "Thanks for inviting me back. I am unsure about the lifeline sponsor, but I'll try it for you."

"That's all I can ask of you, Veronica. Please remember I was you once, so call me anytime you are spiraling out of control."

Vee hugs Ms. Shantae and returns home with a newfound purpose.

She couldn't wait to flip the pages of her diary and ink tonight's submission.

Nympho Log: 26 March 2022

Today, I returned to whore rehab, which was invigorating and intimidating. Especially meeting Asperilla Valdez. I never want to see her in a dark alley. Although, I will admit her dominance is sexy. The meeting allowed me to get close to Devin, who is so fucking fine. I'll continue playing hard to get until he fucks me hard. Nympho out.

She closes the diary, tucks it under her pillow, and retrieves the letter from the envelope. She reads the lame instructions for checking in daily, GPS locations, and medical treatment.

FLENARDO

Her eyes widen at the bottom of the letter, which reads, *most improved whore can win a million-dollar cash prize.*

With that money, she could enroll back in school, bankroll her settlement interest, and achieve her dreams of becoming an FBI agent.

Chapter 6

After a long week of completing contracts and making his clients rich, Devin can finally leave work behind for the weekend. He's excited about the pussy link he paid Asperilla for before she left town.

He rolls his thumb over the screen, searching for women's images on the menu. He slides his thumb faster and knocks the phone down to the floor.

"Damn, I need to slow down before I bust this nut in my pants." He recovers the phone, types in his desires, and awaits a response.

His phone chimes, displaying an address and time for tonight's quest.

He adjusts Devastation to its normal position. "Calm down, fella. I promise you will stroke someone's throat tonight."

He stretches his arms, slides his shirt over his head, and unties the drawstring from his jogging pants.

He stands and trips over his left pants leg while walking toward the bathroom. He stumbles and bangs his head on the wall.

He grabs the counter for leverage, boosts himself up, and sees a bruise above his eyebrow in the mirror.

He laughs and states, "pussy is my downfall."

He turns on the shower and shaves his genitals. He believes pubic hairs slipping between a woman's teeth while she gives head is a sin. Plus, when he beats his dick and shoots cum, it's super easy to rinse off his pelvis and balls.

He wants to munch some pussy and return a lucky female's cum to her mouth. The more money they charge, the more addictive and nastier he will become.

He steps out of the shower and performs oral care. *Floss, brush, rinse*, he recites in his head.

He swishes the mouthwash, spits the overflow in the sink, dries his mouth, and struts to his wardrobe closet.

He chooses a lapel V-neck, blue printed suit with a white open-collar shirt and classic brown leather dress shoes.

He sprays on some Versace cologne and poses in front of the mirror one last time before ordering an Uber.

He goes downstairs and watches the Hawks versus the Knicks game.

DEVASTATION

The Uber app alerts and interrupts the final minutes of the quarter. *Damn, the game was getting good. I'll catch the highlights on SportsCenter,* he thinks to himself.

He slips a handful of condoms into his pocket, sets the house alarm, and walks out the door to approach his driver.

"Mr. Williams?" he asked.

"Yes. The one and only," he announces as he sits in the back seat.

"Sir, do you mind switching your playlist to anything with Jhene Aiko?" Devin asks.

The drivers oblige, and the first song plays.

Devin snaps his finger and hums along.

Thirty minutes later, he arrives in front of a dark, eerie parking garage.

The streets were quiet, and he wasn't too sure if the address was correct. He pulls out his phone and verifies that he's at the right location.

He shrugs his shoulders and creeps into the garage, checking his surroundings with every step. *Where is everyone?* he thinks.

A baritone voice announces in the dark, "you wanna see some ass?"

He remembers the last text from Asperilla and responds, "let me see some cash."

The stranger flashes a beam of light across Devin's face. He squints his eyes and hears the words, "follow me."

The man leads him to the rear of the garage and knocks on a hidden door with a three-knock code.

The door slides open, revealing a tow yard with wrecked cars. Devin pauses in his track and grinds his teeth. "Excuse me, where are we going?"

The unknown man flashes his light across a manhole, frustrating Devin's demeanor even more.

Devin snatches the man by his shirt and pulls him up face to face. "I didn't come here to play games. I came to buy pussy. Now stop fucking with me before I snap your neck and toss you down to the sewer with the turtles."

"Let me go; I was joking. The lady that invited you here thought you would enjoy it."

"What, lady?"

"Asper—something."

"You mean Asperilla?"

"Yeah, that's her name. It was her idea to do this."

"That bitch is demonic. Never listen to anything she says. Take me to get some pussy before you see the dark side of me."

They return to the garage and walk down an unfinished hallway. At the end of the corner, the unknown man presses a button, illuminating the hall and displaying an elevator.

"Mr. William, everything you desire has a floor number. Just push a button."

Devin walks in and stares at all the lustful floors. He feels like a five-year-old kid in a candy store.

"Fuck it! I'll start at the bottom and work my way to the top."

He presses the button for Hedonism, leans against the wall, and anticipates the view.

The doors slide open, inviting him into the smell of sex and the sounds of music.

He rushes to the bar and orders the stiffest drink to calm his nerves from Asperilla's foolishness.

He receives his drink, takes a sip, and scans the room to find someone's daughter or mother to fuck.

Soft fingers trail the back of his neck. He closes his eyes and prays it's a woman since every sexuality is inside this room.

He shivers from a salivating tongue rolling on his vertebrates, followed by the pecks of wet lips.

He inhales the sweet-scented fragrance, spins around, and sees a sexy slim, thick brown woman with shoulder-length hair.

He interlocks his fingers with hers, stands, and spins her in a three-sixty. He admires her rolled-up long-sleeve shirt, revealing cleavage, with one side tucked in the denim shorts and the other hanging down.

He slides back the barstool beside him and invites her for a drink. Her thighs grip her shorts, forcing them to rise a few inches as she sits.

His eyes drift to the tattoo on her inner thighs and how it curves and disappears inside her shorts.

She snaps her fingers. "Can you look at me before I allow you to taste?"

He smiles and rolls his lips. "Excuse my rude manners." He extends his hands. "My name is Devin. And you are?" he asks.

"Tonight, you can call me Armocita."

"Can I call you attractive, reassuring, motivated, original, calm, inventiveness, teach, and aggressive?"

She smiles and asks, "did you break down my name?"

"I sure did because you are a visionary and want success in its deepest meaning. Speaking of vision, I couldn't help but notice your tattoo."

DEVASTATION

"Do you like it?"

"Like it? I want to sink my teeth in your inner thigh. Suck and bite on the spiral designs until you beg me to stop." He pinches her thigh. "How deep does your tattoo goes?"

She hikes her shorts, allowing him to see more of the ostentatious twists and rosettes tattoo resting inches from her hip socket.

The ink compliments her skin. If her pussy lips could speak, would they ask what my mouth does?

He leans in, kisses her bottom lip, and wrestles his tongue with hers to determine the best kisser.

Once satisfied with the victory, he pulls back, smiles, and asks, "would you like to get out of here?"

"Sure, but let me see your phone first."

He thought her request was unusual but slid the phone into her hand.

She snaps a selfie of them together, types in a number, and returns the phone. "My best friend is a police officer, and I never make moves without her knowing. You can never be too careful with people these days. I love to fuck, but my safety is important as well."

She latches on his arms, and he escorts her through the crowd and toward the elevator.

He feels someone watching them from his peripheral vision. He notices Vee drinking and flirting with a couple of men.

Devin ignores his rehab partner because he only wants to wake up tomorrow with his face between Armocita's thighs.

DEVASTATION

Chapter 7

The night is young, and Vee needs some dick.

Especially after seeing Devin leave with some weak pussy.

Bitch walks like her shit is dry, she assumes to herself.

A gentleman places the palm of his hand on Vee's shoulder. "Would you like another drink? This is the second time I offered, but it seems your mind is elsewhere."

"No, I'm fine. Please order me a Gin Negroni. Make that a double and keep them coming until I ask you to stop."

The gentleman passes the first drink to her, and she gulps it down and licks her tongue around the rim of the glass.

She yanks the gentlemen's tie, forcing him to lean onto her. "Tell me your name," she demands.

"Robert."

"That's a simple ass name."

"I beg your pardon?" he says.

"Calm down, Robert. You are too uptight. If you want this pussy, you have to loosen up more. It's not like you have to work for it. You are cute, and I need some dick and tongue tonight. Can you accommodate me?"

"Are you always this aggressive?"

She swallows another drink, slams the glass on the counter, and leaves Robert at the bar.

She leaves the party and walks toward the elevator door. She presses the button and waits for the doors to open.

The door slides open, and a sexy couple is kissing and groping each other. The man winks his eye at Vee, and she already knows he wants to add her to the equation.

She drops to her knees, unzips his pants, and slides his dick through the zipper. Her eyes widen as the uncircumcised dick stares into her eyes, daring her to kiss it. She pushes the foreskin back, licking the precum oozing from his urethral meatus.

"Umm, you taste so fucking good," she moans. "Fingerfuck your bitch while I suck your dick."

The woman lifts her skirt and reveals she is panty-less. Her pussy lips were huge, and she appeared freshly waxed. Vee breaks from sucking the man's dick to stealing a few licks on the tip of his girlfriend's clitoris.

Vee grabs his hands and glides them into his girlfriend's swollen wet pussy.

"Deeper, Stefan," the woman gasps.

The transformation of Steve Urkel was the first thought inside of Vee's head when she heard Stefan.

She giggles to herself and returns her attention to Stefan's dick.

She strokes his dick through the palm of her hand, pulling back and forth until it stands erect and robust.

Sliding a strand of her hair behind her ear, she opens her mouth, licking the tip of his head, and swallows him whole, bobbing her neck up and down.

Stefan grabs the back of her head and burrows his dick farther down her throat.

He yanks his girlfriend by the hair, "Bitch, kiss me."

She opens her mouth, and he spits on her tongue. "Lisa, you like that nasty shit, huh? Kiss me harder while I fuck this hoe's throat."

Lisa does as he commands, biting his lips and neck, sucking on his earlobe while jabbing her fingers in her wet pussy.

The elevator door slides open, and Vee notices a voyeuristic couple watching, and she doesn't want to disappoint them.

Vee presses her hands between the door to prevent them from closing.

She gets up, faces the couple, and turns her head over her shoulder, "Stefan, fuck me hard so our guests can enjoy the threesome."

He runs over, lifts her skirt, and slides his dick inside her. Vee moans, wipes her tongue on her fingers, and plays with her clit as he continues to thrust harder.

"Yeah, fuck this pussy. Yes, yes, yes."

She gyrates her hips in a circular motion while he slaps her ass cheeks.

He looks at Lisa and yells, "this bitch's pussy is juicy as fuck. I'm going to let you suck the creampie out of her when I'm done nutting."

Lisa anticipates the flavor and runs her finger over her clitoris ferociously.

Stefan goes deeper as his balls flap against Vee's skin.

"Cum in me, Stefan," Vee moans.

He grips her shoulder for extra leverage and hammers his dick faster than before.

Together they produce the best clapping sound intertwined with heavy breathing.

He turns his head and watches Lisa pinches her nipples and penetrates herself with three fingers.

"Oh shit, this is the best night of my life!" he expresses.

He rams Vee's pussy, biting his lip, and slaps her ass cheeks.

"I'm cumming, hoe. Hold still and take this dick."

Vee loves a dirty-talking man, and her pussy becomes wetter than before. She knows she is about to squirt but holds it until Stefan cums.

Stefan digs more profound into her pussy as she cries for more.

He pulls his dick out, and Vee spanks her clit before inserting more fingers.

Stefan watched Lisa and Vee masturbate and didn't want to be alone. He beats his dick and grunts at the couple outside the elevator.

His hands tremble, and as he is ready to cum, he slams his dick inside Vee's sloppy wet pussy.

After he nuts, he slides his dick out, staggers, and regains his balance before sitting on the floor.

He watches cum drip from Vee's swollen lips and points his fingers at Lisa.

"Go suck out your dessert," he instructs.

Lisa crawls onto the elevator floor, opens her mouth, and sucks Stefan's cum from Vee's pussy.

The voyeuristic couple claps their hands and thanks them for the show.

Vee knows the party isn't complete until she releases a nut. She sits on Lisa's face and slowly grinds her pussy over her nose and mouth.

Lisa flicks her tongue over Vee's clit.

"Ooh, ooh, ooh," Vee moans.

She grabs Lisa's hair and rides her face harder.

"Umm, umm," she moans.

Lisa sucks her clit harder.

Vee leans her head back, loudly moans, and squirts all over Lisa's face.

Vee's head spins in circles, and she takes a moment to regain her serenity.

"Oh shit, you two were incredible. Stefan, take my number. Never know, a threesome in the zoo might be on the horizon."

Her outfit has wet spots, and her hair is jumbled, but she is satisfied; that is all that matters right now.

Even after a spontaneous threesome and a mind-blowing orgasm, she wishes it could have been with Devin.

She presses the button to take her to the garage floor but is not in the mood to go home yet.

DEVASTATION

She drives to Moonrise Hotel since they are open until one-thirty in the morning.

She parks her car, dances into the hotel, and rides the elevator to the rooftop bar for more alcohol.

"What will it be, ma'am?" the bartender asks.

"Surprise me," she replies.

She admires the rooftop scene, wondering who's in love and who's just fucking.

She believes in the motto, *fuck them before they fuck you.* All her ex's either abused or stole from her. Love is for fairy tales, so the only happy ending she will ever experience is the high from an orgasm.

"Excuse me, ma'am, your drink is here," the bartender interrupts.

She sips and rolls her tongue over her upper lip to attract the bartender.

"What do you call this?"

"Naked and Famous. A mixture of banhez mezal, aperol, yellow chartreuse, and lemon," he describes.

"I'm not sure what you are talking about, but I love how it tastes. By the way, I'll never be famous, but I can be naked once your shift ends."

He smiles and winks his eye. "Ma'am, I'll be back. I have to serve my other customers before I get fired."

FLENARDO

She admires his ass through his black slacks.

She sips her drink and thinks, *two dicks in one night. I better get all I can before I lock myself in a cocoon to win this money.*

DEVASTATION

Chapter 8

Armocita shivers from the cold temperature in the room. She scoots toward the middle of the bed, searching for a warm body to cuddle with.

It only takes a few inches for her to realize she is lying alone. "I can't believe he left me in bed sleep and didn't even wake me to say good morning.

"Well, fuck him! Where the fuck is Devastation? That dick had my heart, ass, pussy, and mouth wide open."

She throws her hands in the air and shuffles her feet in the sheets from the frustration of not getting a morning orgasm.

She rolls out the bed, slips on a T-shirt, and searches the condo for Devin.

She passes his study area and reads the descriptions of his accolades. Not only can he fuck, but he's intelligent, talented, and successful.

She snoops through the condo and finds a room with a cracked door. She peeps inside and sees Devin riding a Peloton with his eyes close.

He has on ear buds and never notices Armocita standing at the door. She observes his dick bouncing against his thigh as he slowly pedals the bike.

His workout is turning her on, and she wants to fuck. She can replace morning breath with cum wash.

She lifts her shirt, slides her fingers in her moist pussy, and clamps her thighs together.

She bites her lip and moans, "damn. I need to ride his face before I leave."

As she fiddles with her lips, she trips and lands on her face.

He jumps from the bike, dick swinging as he extends a hand to help her up.

Feeling embarrassed, she slaps his dick and yells, "get that monster away from me."

He lifts and carries her to the wall. He stoops down, spreads her legs, and eats her from behind.

She opens her ass cheeks wider and smears her wetness over his face.

"Give me all your tongue. Sink it in deep," she moans.

He obliges and continues substituting his morning breakfast for a bowl of orgasms.

"Fuck me on your bike!" she screams.

He leads her to the bike and lifts her on his lap. She glides his dick in and wraps her legs around his waist.

He pedals slowly, and his thrusts inside of her are at the same speed.

"Damn, this pussy feels good. Can you ride this dick faster?"

"I thought you'd never ask," she responds.

She wraps her arms around his shoulder blades, lifts and drops down, slapping her ass cheeks on his thighs.

"Armocita, you going to make me bust this nut in you."

She stares into his eyes. "That's fine, and you will eat it out of me too."

He lifts her off the bike and makes her grab the handlebars. "I'm about to beat your pussy from the back, hard as fuck."

"Give it to me then. I like pain."

He inserts his dick and tunnels like a runaway train with no breaks. He pulls her hair, forcing her to turn her head around and kiss him.

He inserts two fingers in her pussy as he fucks her harder and harder.

His body trembles as he slams his dick into her walls.

He takes another stroke, releases his nut, and falls over on her back.

"Oh, no, Muthafucker, a promise is a promise."

She slides aways from him and lies on the yoga mat with her legs and toes pointing toward the ceiling.

Devin dives in and licks his load, anticipating her cumming momentarily.

He inserts his middle finger into her asshole, and she moans as he sucks her lips.

"Deeper, baby. Eat and finger my ass deeper," she cries.

The wetness from her pussy runs into his eyes, but he refuses to stop until she cums.

He rolls his tongue circularly over her clit and jabs her asshole deeper as requested.

It didn't take long for her to cum and push his face away.

He stands and wipes his face. "I'm going to start the shower. I'll see you in a few minutes."

Armocita stares at the ceiling and can't wait to brag to her BFF about being fucked and eaten to infinity.

Her pussy twitched from the pleasure, and she could stay here forever if she didn't have to work today.

She rolls over, pushes to lift from the ground, and strolls into the bathroom.

"Did you leave any hot water for me?"

DEVASTATION

"Yes, and I have shower gel, a cap for your hair, and lotion in the closet."

She shrugs her shoulder from the odd remark and checks out his selections.

She selects the bio almond body wash, a kitsch shower caps, and a milk & honey whipped body butter.

Never in her life had she seen a man with more feminine products than her. Is he bisexual, into drag, or just fucking a lot of bitches?

He comes out of the shower with his dick swinging again. "All yours. I'm going downstairs to prepare breakfast. How do you like your eggs?"

"Wow, you beat pussy and eggs?" she jokes.

"There's a lot you don't know about me. We can chat while we eat."

He kisses her cheek, dries off, and exits the bathroom.

She slides in the shower and realizes she has no clothes to wear home.

The bathroom closet has rows of feminine products, so I know he has a woman's short set available.

She finishes her shower and tiptoes into the bedroom. The smell of bacon lingers under her nose, and she can't wait to see what else he's cooking.

On the bed are an oversized T-shirt and a note.

Please slip this cute shirt on and join me for breakfast.

She shrugs her shoulders, smiles, and follows the instructions.

She makes her way downstairs, and her eyes widen. She places her palm over her mouth. French toast with bananas, crispy bacon, and scrambled eggs with cheese was on the table.

He runs over, escorts her to her seat, and kisses her neck.

He places a glass of orange juice and champagne beside her plate.

"To us and many more memories." He lifts his glass and clings it against hers.

"Devin, I think you are moving too fast," she informs.

"Not at all. I truly like you, and please don't choke on your French toast because this conversation is about to get real, upfront, and raw. I love women, but I don't trust easily due to past relationships."

He hands her a white envelope. "Go ahead, open it."

Her eyebrows raise out of curiosity. "I hope you aren't about to reveal you have HIV or used to be a woman."

He squeezes his dick through his pants. "No, ma'am. I'm all man, and I get tested weekly."

She opens the envelope, and her stomach flutters after seeing ten crisp one-hundred dollars bills.

"Devin, I'm confused. Why are you giving me money? Is this a *50 Shades of Grey* contract? I'm not into that."

"As I stated before, I like you. I like buying... No, I love buying pussy because, mentally, it allows me to fuck beautiful women and not catch feelings."

She looks at the money, looks at Devin, and then looks at the money again to make sure she's not dreaming.

"Are you going to cook every morning after we fuck?"

"Sure, when we fuck in the house, but are you willing to become my addiction?"

"Hell yeah! I have student loans to pay off," she replies. "I only have one concern. Will I be the only woman?"

"No, but I will use protection and produce my health records before we engage in any activity. I will never kiss or perform oral with another woman."

"Devin, you are one of the most charming freaks I have ever met."

"Armocita, do we have a deal?"

"Yes but call me Cupcakes."

"Why is that?"

"Because you will eat the cream out of my chocolate ass."

He sips his drinks and places the glass on the table. He responds with a wicked smile and winks his eye, "I'll pay extra for that shit. Now eat your breakfast because I don't want you blaming me for you being late for work."

"No, I will never blame you, but I forgot to mention one last thing. I won't sit around and wait for you to call or skip dates."

"I'm a fucking planner. You will know well in advance when I need you. I'll never become jealousy or interrupt your social life."

She looks at her money again and responds, "yes, we have a deal. Can you crawl under the table and eat my pussy while I eat these eggs?"

He drops to his knees and looks up. "Breakfast and head is my expertise."

DEVASTATION

Chapter 9

Vee sips coffee while walking through her kitchen fully nude. She whistles, and Joe Joe races into the room and mounts the side of her leg. His nub wags back and forth, and his tongue flaps nonstop.

She rubs his head, "are you ready to eat?"

He jumps and sits beside his feeding bowl, awaiting his morning treat and breakfast.

She claps her hands together and says, "eat."

She turns around, walks into the living room, and allows Joe Joe to destroy his meal in peace.

She grabs her phone and texts Ms. Shantae; *I'm not cut out for this mission. Devin hates me, and we cannot have a regular dialogue without arguing over bullshit.*

She taps her nails over the screen while waiting impatiently for Ms. Shantae's responses.

The word *read* appears on the screen, and now she's excited and nervous simultaneously.

Ms. Shantae replies, *please meet me tomorrow in my office at 6 pm. Don't be late.*

What the hell? Why the fucking suspense?

Ok. I'll be there, Vee texts back.

She places the phone on the charger and grabs her journal to ink another juicy story.

Nympho Log: 5 April 2022

Last night, I had a threesome in an elevator with Stefan and Lisa. We had an audience who loved seeing us suck, fuck, and lust over each other. Just when you thought my night was over, I fucked a bartender, and he was full of surprises. He created a makeshift bed on the floor with pillows from the lounge chairs. I rode and drained his dick until the sun cracked the sky and beamed on our naked skin. I think I'll have a drink later tonight. Nympho out.

She places the journal on the table and silently counts *5, 4, 3, 2, and 1* in her head. The doorbell rings and her pussy clench as she opens the door.

Outside, leaning against the wall, is Jonathan's brother, Kevon.

He grabs and tugs his dick through his jogging pants. "My brother said you were looking for all of this."

She licks her lips and pulls him inside. "You better allow me to get mine first, unlike your selfish ass brother."

"No worries. I promise to make sure you cum first."

"Mmm, I can't wait to feel you inside of me. Fucking me deep and hard. We won't need the bedroom. Bend me over the kitchen island," she insists.

Kevon lifts his shirt over his head and slides his jogging pants and underwear down to his knees. He grips his shaft and slides it through the palm of his hand as the length and thickness erect.

Vee spreads her legs, leans over the island, and grabs her Cum Snatcher, her nickname for her portable rose. She turns on the powerful suction and glides it over clit.

She turns her head over her shoulder. She jerks and stutters her words. "Fuckkkkkk meeee nowww."

Kevon reaches around her waist and cups his hands around hers and the rose. "Vee, your nasty ass is going to get this dick."

The tip of his dick pierces her from behind, and she feels rejuvenated with every inch.

He grips the rose tighter as her walls clench around his dick. "Ooh, that's it. Fuck me, Daddy."

He slams his dick in and out as her ass cheeks bounce against his thighs.

"Ooh, shit," she moans. "Harder, Kevon! Give it to me harder."

He releases the rose, latches his hands around her waist, and fucks her like the nasty slut she wants to be.

He slaps her ass cheeks and fucks her faster and deeper.

"You asked for this morning's dick and are getting this muthafucker. Hurry up and cum, you dirty hoe. Cum on my dick, bitch!"

She holds the rose firmly as she takes the inches from Kevon. It doesn't take long for her orgasm to reach its peak.

"Give it to me, Kevon. Don't fucking stop. I'm there."

He grunts and pounds her harder, pressing her head on the island counter. His slob slides from his mouth and drips onto the middle of her back.

He lifts her in the air and flips her around. She throws her legs in the air and keeps Cum Snatcher's intensity going.

Kevon spreads her ass cheeks and slides his tongue in between them.

"Umm, I'm about to cum, baby. That's my spot."

She closes her eyes as her body shivers. The rose hums, and Kevon's tongue punches into her asshole.

"Ahh, ahh," she moans. Her hips rock upwards. "Ooh, ooh, ooh."

Kevon comes up for air and slides his dick in her pussy. "You're going to squirt on this muthafucka," he instructs.

He slides his dick in and out of her as her moans become louder.

As soon as she releases her grip on the rose, she squirts like a lightning bolt.

"Give me this nut. Give me this nut!" he yells as he slaps her ass cheeks harder while ravishing her pussy.

She breathes harder and continues to bang her ass against his thighs.

"I'm cumming, bitch. Give me this pussy."

"Take it. It's yours."

He thrusts a few more seconds, pulls his dick out, and ejaculates over her breast and stomach.

He walks backward, trips over his pants, and falls on the floor.

She laughs before asking, "are you okay?"

"Yes. Between the squirting, the rose, and your moist pussy, I lost myself for a moment."

She laughs at the situation, spreads her legs, and glides two fingers over her swollen lips. "See? My pussy is not to be fucked with."

"Yeah, I know."

"Can a man wash your juicy off?"

"Sure."

"Turn on my shower and bring me a hot towel to clean your kids off my stomach."

He returns, wipes her down quickly, and lifts her from the counter.

"Where's the cleaning or disinfectant spray?"

"Don't worry. I'll wipe the counter after you leave."

"Damn, my dick isn't as good as you say if you are sending me home already."

She punches him in the arm. "Your dick is worth its weight in gold, but we know I'm only good for a fuck. Plus, you need to head back home before your girlfriend calls and asks what's taking you so long at the store."

His phone rings instantly.

"See? She has a tracking device on you. Get out of here before she knocks on my door."

"You never wanted me as a husband, and you're still fucking my brother."

"That little dick muthafucka? He's a waste of time."

His phone rings again.

"Vee, hold on. Let me answer this call."

"Go ahead. I'm going to shower and watch *Criminal Minds*. Lock the door behind you."

"Vee, what we share used to be special."

"We have special sex; I'll call when I need it, and you better come running."

"Well, I won't be able to come much longer."

"Why not?"

"Because I'm getting engaged, and I'm going to be faithful to her."

"Yeah, right, that's my dick."

"Vee, I'm serious this time."

"Kevon, get the fuck out of my house with that bullshit."

She leaves him standing in the kitchen and walks to the bathroom to shower.

The water is refreshing, and she erases the conversation with Kevon with memories of Devin.

She closes her eyes and imagines waking up to him in the morning. *Tomorrow, I'll be nice when I meet him. Maybe he will give in and let me suck his dick in the parking lot.*

FLENARDO

DEVASTATION

Chapter 10

Vee's body has been tingling nonstop since Ms. Shantae informed her that Devin would be attending the meeting. She wears a multicolored sundress without panties and some adorable purple pumps.

She enters the building and notices the polished designer tiles reflecting her image as she walks down the hall.

She approaches a group of people passing out flyers with the words, "you are not alone."

She collects a flyer, flips it around, and discovery the diverse self-help classes. For a small moment, she realizes everyone is facing or fighting demons.

"Thanks for the flyer," she replies as she smiles and continues to Ms. Shantae's class.

She taps two times on the door, announcing her presence before entering the meeting. She becomes lost for words once her eyes trial to the imprint in Devin's hoochie daddy shorts.

"Veronica, are you ok?" Ms. Shaunte asks.

"Yeah, a little distracted, but all is well."

"Good! Please have a seat, and let's get this meeting underway. First, I know you dislike each other, but we are a team striving for victory. Abstinence and control don't arrive overnight. Change requires time and baby steps."

Devin raises his hand, "excuse me, Ms. Shaunte. Have you ever been addicted or hurt?"

"Yes, I have, but my story is more complex. It was either transformation or jail. I was facing sexual assault charges for forcing my ex-husband to fuck me. Excuse my language. I meant to say forcing him to have sex with me. The Ph.D. can't hide my hood side forever."

She chuckles for a quick second and returns to her serious mode.

"Okay, enough about me and my past. Let's discuss your homework assignment. Tonight, you all are going on a date."

Ms. Shantae turns her head toward, "and Vee, no sex."

"Why are you acting like I'm the only one fucking? Devin's in the rehab too," Vee said.

"Yeah, but my addiction is stable; you are a fucking nympho," Devin states.

"Your bank account isn't stable. I'm sure it's wide open and being constantly withdrawn from, over all the pussy you are buying."

"Enough!" Ms. Shantae shouts. "You two act like children. Listen, you are going out tonight, and your homework is due at the end of the week.

"Class dismissed," she announces.

Devin yanks one of his locs before standing and extending his hand to Vee. "Let's go before I change my mind."

Vee's stomach churns from the initial contact of her tiny fingers sliding between Devin's dark, smooth hands.

They say their goodbyes to Ms. Shantae and walk down the hallway.

They play along until they step outside the building. Vee stares at the blue and orange sky, making love together. "Isn't this romantic, Devin? Our first sunset."

Devin shakes his hand loose from hers. "Bitch, let me go. I'm still pissed at you. You threw your coffee on me."

"It was a latte, and are you driving, or shall I?"

"I don't have a car," he admits.

"Oh my. You are full of surprises, Mr. Devin Williams. Damn, you spend that much on pussy that you can't even buy a Chevrolet Spark?" she jokes.

"I can call an Uber, but feel free to drive, Ms. Veronica Hemsley."

"Follow me. We are going to have so much fun tonight."

Vee presses her key fob and unlocks the doors while they walk toward her car.

Devin places his hands around Vee's waist, slides her left, and opens the door. Devin's mannerisms caught Vee off guard, and she wasn't sure how to respond.

She stands dazed for a few seconds.

"Vee, get your crazy ass in the car."

"Yes, of course. Thank you for opening my door."

They drove away, and neither of them spoke for ten minutes. No music was playing, and Devin refused to ride in silence.

"Are you originally from St. Louis?" Devin asks to break up the awkward ride.

"No, I'm originally from South Florida. Yourself?"

"I'm from down South as well. Alabama, to be exact."

"Roll Tide, Roll," she shouts.

"I'm too busy for the rivalry. I'm neutral about football and their teams. By the way, where are we going?"

"To one of my favorite places to pick up men. BB's Jazz, Blues, and Soup," she answers.

"Well, you won't need a man tonight since I'm your date."

"True," she agrees.

She continues driving while engaging in small talk until they reach their destination.

Once again, Devin hops out of the car and opens her door.

"Mr. Devin, if I didn't know better, I'd say you are being nice to me."

"Don't flatter yourself, Vee. I'm a whore with manners. Let's get in here because I'm hungry as hell."

The closer they walk towards the entrance, the better they can hear the blues from inside welcoming them into the restaurant.

Vee notices Devin bobbing his head with every step.

They enter, and Vee requests a table for two.

The hostess looks at her seating chart and grabs two menus. "Please follow me."

She leads them to a booth in the corner, where they can see the band up close.

"This is a nice view. How often do you come here?"

"Maybe three times a week. I have a personal bathroom stall where I give head and ass."

"What the fuck!"

"Calm down, Devin. I'm messing with you."

"I need a drink because you are working my nerves with all this sex talk," he admits.

A waitress says, "welcome to BB's. Are you guys ready to order?"

"Sure. Can I start with some smoked salmon cakes?" he asks.

"Yuck!" Vee, open her mouth and demonstrates throwing up. "You're not about to eat that in front of me," she states.

"Vee, be quiet. Order something to drink and stop embarrassing me."

"No worries, we are used to Vee's crazy ass in here," the hostess said.

"While he's ordering the fishy shit, can you please bring me a Heineken, one goose island, and a Corona?"

"Sir, would you like to order a drink as well?"

"It appears she's ordered the entire drink menu," he jokes.

"Please bring me a glass of Moscato if you don't mind."

"Gotcha. I'll be back shortly with your drinks and appetizers."

"Why did you order three drinks at once?"

"I love to drink and fuck. Oh, and sometimes I'll pop a pill and fuck, smoke, and fuck, or just fuck and fuck. A girl has needs."

"Listen, Vee. I also have needs, and I love to fuck, but listening to you talk about it all the time is annoying. Let's enjoy this vibe tonight and get through our first homework assignment."

"You're no fun, but okay. Have it your way."

The band continues playing, and Devin tunes Vee's conversation out until the server returns with their order.

"Here you all go. Will there be anything else?" she asks.

"No, we're fine for now," Devin said.

Vee turns her head away from Devin's salmon, and slams the first drink down her throat, followed by the second and third.

Devin cuts into his salmon and chews his dinner like he eats pussy. He slices again, glides the fork in the air, and suggests Vee try some.

She politely declines and waves to the servers. "Another round for me, please. If I'm going to throw-up, it won't be from that fish," she said.

The server laughs and tells Vee she will return with her drinks.

Devin notices Vee's dimples and green eyes. He scrolls farther down, makes a mental note of her breast, and wonders if they are implants.

"Ooh, someone is watching me," Vee said.

His lips curl and form a smile. "Not really. I was reading your shirt."

She tilts her head, stretches the shirt, and reads, "Freak in the sheets. Killer on the streets."

"At least the shirt is cool," he comments. "By the way, you owe me an apology for throwing your latte on me."

"You are right."

I want to throw this pussy on you, she thinks to herself.

"I apologize for being an ass when we first met."

"Apology accepted. Let's enjoy this evening, and I'll even have a drink or two with your throat-baby ass," he jokes.

The music, food, and drinks set a great vibe as they engaged in deeper conversation until the bar closed.

Chapter 11

Vee opens her eyes and jumps from her sleeping position in the bed. She glances around the room and notices picture frames and plants that don't belong to her. She panics and screams, "help, help, somebody help me!" at the top of her lungs.

Devin rushes through the door and yells, "calm your ass down. You are screaming like someone is trying to rape your ass in here. I'm not going to jail for you if the neighbors call the police. You're lucky I brought your ass home instead of allowing the two guys to slut you out. You were on the dance floor, flashing titties and dry humping every man and woman close to you."

"Devin, I apologize, and thanks for looking out for me." She closes her eyes and slides the cover down to her knees.

"Vee, what the fuck are you doing now? You are strange as hell. I'm two seconds away from putting you out."

She opens her eyes and is relieved she's wearing panties, and no moisture is running between her thighs.

"Whew! Thanks a lot for not taking advantage of a drunk bitch. Usually, a guy would fuck and throw me in an Uber before sunrise."

"Drunk pussy is for sloppy muthafuckers, and apparently, those are the guys you attract."

"Well, excuse me. That says a lot from a guy that can only get pussy if he swipes a credit card."

"Look, Vee. I'm not in the mood for your shit. I'm surprised no one reported a black man aiding a white woman out of the bar last night. Excuse me for cleaning the vomit off your clothes. You were drunk as a skunk, and you weren't about to lie in my bed all nasty and shit."

"Aww, you did all that for me?" Vee blinks her lashes and smiles.

He points toward the ottoman at the foot of the bed. "There's your washed and folded clothes, toiletries, and personal belongings. Once you finish, come downstairs so I can feed you and send you home."

He closes the door and leaves Vee to herself.

Who the hell does he think he's talking to? she thinks.

He's a little aggressive this morning. That can only mean one thing. She snaps her fingers and sings a made-up song, "good dick and deep strokes. Always swallow and never choke," on her way to the shower.

DEVASTATION

She loves the layout of Devin's bathroom and dreams of having something similar. She adjusts the temperature of the water, and jazz music plays instantly.

Oh, he's a classic muthafucker, she thinks to herself while dancing to the tune.

She places her foot on the ledge, retrieves the shower head, and sprays the stream of water on her clit.

She moans and gently lifts the tip of her hood and traces slow circles for intense pleasure. She closes her eyes, thinks of Devin, and cums three times in a row.

Once satisfied, she cleanses, washes her hair, and prepares to get dressed.

She feels awkward because she stayed over a man's house after one date, and they didn't fuck. She rushes downstairs to inquire about last night's encounter.

She is about to ask Devin if he is gay, but the bacon and eggs aroma shifts her focus elsewhere.

She imagines Devin cooking and wearing nothing but an apron. Perfect round ass cheeks, delicious pecs, biceps, and forearms tighten as he scrambles the eggs.

The sound of the plate being placed on the table disturbs her moment. "Here you go, Vee. I hope you enjoy your breakfast."

She digs her fork into the eggs and takes a big bite. "Mmm, you are awesome in the kitchen. I might catch an orgasm from this breakfast."

She bites the crispy bacon and begins to speak and eat. "Devin, are you gay? Because I'm fine, I sleep in sexy lingerie, and my eyes are mesmerizing. You gotta be out of your mind not to fuck me."

"Vee, I peep some of your qualities, but nymphos aren't my cup of tea. We are in rehab for a reason, and I'm sure Ms. Shantae would disapprove of her students fucking each other. Plus, you know my addiction. I only buy pussy when I need a nut. It's safer for my heart," he explains.

"Yes, but it has to be exhausting for your bank account," she responds.

He shrugs his shoulders, eats his breakfast, and shuts down the conversation.

After breakfast, Vee offers to wash the dishes to make small talk.

Devin smiles and responds, "sure, I'll never turn down help, but let's do it together. You can wash, and I'll rinse since I have a special spot for my dishes."

"Do you think we passed our first homework assignment?" Vee asks.

DEVASTATION

"Of course! And if we hang out more, we might have a chance to win the million-dollar prize," Devin mentions.

"That is a lot of money, but I'm not sure about winning. During breakfast, I was fantasizing about licking your ass while you were cooking," she admits.

Devin laughs and winks his eye. "Never heard that one before. You are unique," he responds. "You are an incredible woman, and I have a confession. Last night, everything about you was terrific—your choice of perfume, style of clothes, hair, and especially the dimples.

"Once you became the exorcist and threw up, all that shit went out the window. You probably don't remember, but I had to shower with you to clean your ass up."

"You could have just taken the pussy. I wouldn't have accused you of rape. I like the thought of waking up covered in cum."

"Vee, that's sick as fuck. I'm not doing that shit. That's not consent, and you're too pretty to be used as a bottom feeder. It would be best if you decreased your actions with strangers.

"I can't believe I'm sitting here, attempting to make another whore see the light. I'm beginning to think if Jesus came, you would give him head instead of asking for healing. Oh God, I'm already on my knees and ready to serve you," he jokes.

"That isn't funny, Devin. I know my limits, and I wouldn't stoop that low. I've had a rough life, and fucking is all I know," she responds.

He senses the change in her voice and attitude. He reaches out and hugs her before she tears up. "I apologize for the last statement. Sometimes my asshole game is strong."

He invites her into the den and flips on the TV. "Have a seat, and let's watch some Criminal Minds."

"Oh wow! Now you're speaking my language. This is one of my favorite series. What season are you on?"

He noticed her excitement and was happy they had something in common.

"I'm on the final season because I binge-watch every episode at least four times," he responds.

She claps her hand. "You are going to have a hard time getting rid of me now."

He grabs her hands. "Vee, will you accept me as your Criminal Minds' date once a week?"

"Yes, yes, yes!" She dives into his arms and gives him a gigantic hug.

DEVASTATION

She pulls away, but he retrieves her back, "we are going to cuddle and dissect the criminals before the agents do."

She shifts her body and creates a comfortable spot between his legs. She feels protected and happy for the first time in a long time.

Be careful, Devin. You can't allow a woman to get near your heart again. Just enjoy the series and remember she is only a homework assignment, he reminds himself.

FLENARDO

DEVASTATION

Chapter 12

On his way home from work, Devin stops in the lobby, collects his mail, and rides the elevator to his apartment.

Once inside, he sifts through the envelopes, tossing the advertising and junk mail into the trash pile. One letter catches his attention, and he smiles when he realizes it's from Vee.

He opens it and reads, *Thanks for the Criminal Minds' date. Tonight at 7 pm, your presence is requested for a new homework assignment. I'll text you later with the info.*

Signed, your poetic partner in rehab.

"Wow, she could have just texted or called me, but I'm feeling the old-school vibe of sending a letter through the mail."

He checks the time on his Fitbit and realizes it's 6 pm. He runs upstairs, strips out of his clothes, and jumps in the shower.

After scrubbing his balls, face, and body, he brushes his teeth and skips to his wardrobe closet.

FLENARDO

He picks out a sweater, a jean jacket, and white sneakers. He sprays on some Polo Black cologne and slides a fedora over his locs.

He is happy with his attire and can't wait for Vee to see and smell his sexiness. He loves making her smile and enjoys her company, especially since they share a few things in common.

His phone chimes with a message and he assumes it is Vee, but it's Ms. Yu Yan.

He reads the message, and the opportunity to work in Beijing requires a response in less than thirty days.

He debates about staying in St. Louis or choosing a lifestyle of endless pussy and a seven-figure salary. Many of his co-workers have said they would have fled America naked with their dick swinging through TSA.

He responds to the text, *Thanks for the reminder. I'll provide my answer before the deadline.*

He returns to the mirror and licks his lips, saying, "Yup! I'm going to be one of the most desirable bachelors tonight. Pussy will want me, but I'm not slanging dick unless her pussy is worth buying."

As soon as he mentions buying pussy, his thoughts change from Vee to Armocita.

He dials her number, and she answers on the second ring.

"Good evening, Mr. Williams. Are you calling so I can make plans to ride your face?"

He laughs briefly and sends her a Cash App. "Not this time, but soon, real soon."

She tells him about her day and how stressful it was working and studying. He notices the pause in the conversation and how she returns to the phone with excitement.

"Devin, you didn't have to send that money. I need to work for that stack."

"You're good. Go buy yourself something nice; a book, a spa day, or dessert at your favorite restaurant."

"Thank you so much! Next time you call me, you better be ready for me to swallow Devastation's kids."

She moans on the phone and informs him how her pussy is drenched from thinking about his dick.

His phone chimes and interrupts the moment. It's a text from Vee with the location of tonight's adventures.

"Armocita, you have a way of making my dick hard. Our next meet-up will have you in every Kama Sutra position known to man. Please excuse my rudeness, but I have to run. Please remember to treat yourself, and we'll talk again soon."

"Sure thing. I'll be waiting to hear from you. Be safe tonight."

The call ends, and he gathers his belongings and heads out the door.

He enjoys the breeze while waiting on the Uber to arrive. He googles Shameless Ground and discovers the meetup location is a lightweight swinger's bar. The image of the place looks like a brick house on the corner, but the address is only 15 miles from downtown.

"Food, drinks, and sexy music. I'm going to showcase the beast for Vee tonight. She might have to make sure I get home safe and sound tonight. Especially after I get drunk and bury my face in some titties."

The Uber driver arrived while Devin texted Vee that he would be there shortly.

"What's your name, sir?" Devin asks.

"Willie, but all my friends call me Wonka."

"What the fuck! Are you walking around with chocolate and golden tickets?"

Wille laughs and explains how it was a childhood name that grew on him. "Hey, it's a funny name, but the ladies love the chocolate part."

"I can relate to some nicknames. I have one of my own," Devin said.

"Willie, tonight is your lucky night. I'm feeling good and hope you will after I tip you for the ride. Money has a purpose, and I want you to use the tip to buy the best piece of pussy in St. Louis."

Devin taps the back seat. "I'm talking about that Harlem Night Sunshine pussy. Do you hear me, Mr. Wonka?"

Willie laughs and informs Devin that he's a faithful married man.

"Fuck that. It's a Devastation type night! You are going to call your wife and role-play. Call her right now and put her on speakerphone," Devin demands.

"Sir, I can't."

"No such word. Be spontaneous for once and put some fire into your marriage. I have a five-hundred-dollar tip if you do it."

"Man, you better not be fucking with me. I could use the extra cash."

"My word is truth. Hurry up before I reach my destination."

Willie facetime his wife, and Devin hijacks the video call.

"Good evening, Mrs. Wonka. My name is Devin. I need you to be butt naked at the door when Willie comes home tonight. I have five hundred dollars for you and him if you can turn back the clock and fuck like jackrabbits."

"Willie, who are you riding with, and is he serious?"

"He's serious, baby. Weird but serious," Wille mentions.

"Okay. Well, bring your ass home after you drop him off."

She disconnects the video, and Willie accelerates faster to his destination.

As the Uber stops in front of Shameless Ground, Devin keeps his word and tips a stack to the driver.

He pounds fist with Willie. "I better hear ya'll fucking from here tonight."

He walks away from the car and enters the place, not as Devin Williams but as Devastation. He locates Vee and hugs her. "Thanks for the invite. Are you ready to fuck up some shit?"

"What in the world are you on, Devin? I have never seen you this wide open before, but I love it!"

"This is the Gemini side of me, and I barely allow him to come out and party with peasants. Therefore, everyone

DEVASTATION

here better appreciate this moment for the rest of their lives."

FLENARDO

Chapter 13

Vee decides to use a straw instead of downing her drink, hoping the slow sipping will keep her from getting intoxicated.

She forces a fake smile when a gentleman asks, "is that your friend over there? He's drinking enough for everyone in the bar."

She observes Devin putting his mouth on an unknown woman's breast. To prevent embarrassment, she walks over, pulls his hair, and his mouth retracts from her titty.

"Devin, what the fuck are you doing? Sucking a woman's titty in the bar is not a part of the homework assignment."

"Well, why did you bring me here?"

"We are here to observe people's sex addictions and how it makes them act irresponsibly in public. You are supposed to be the responsible one. Tonight, be my sponsor, not a dick-slanging demon."

He playfully slaps the right side of his cheeks and then the left. "Alright, Vee. I'm back to my usual self. I thought you would love my wild side."

He hugs her and escorts her to the table. "Let's complete this homework assignment so you can stop busting my balls."

As soon as they sit, she pulls up the whore rehab app on her phone and initiates the conversations. "The assignment says we are meeting a unicorn," she reads.

"Are you talking about a white horse with horns and a multi-colored tail? I had no idea they were real. Damn, tonight is going to be unimaginable. I'm going to ride that bitch."

"Devin, you are tipsy. I'm not speaking about a real unicorn. I'm referring to a single person in a swinger or polyamorous relationship."

"Boo. Boring," he responds.

He sips a drink, stands, and imitates galloping while singing, "If you wanna ride, ride the white pony."

He quits clowning once a cute Hawaiian chick in an orange dress with white polka dots, and tan leather heels approach their table. Her long jet-black hair stops at the lower part of her back.

"Aloha, my name is Naomi."

Her perky titties catch his eye, and his greeting takes longer than usual.

Vee snaps her fingers, and Devin pays attention.

DEVASTATION

He leans in and kisses Naomi's hand. "Excuse my manner. You are an exquisite being. I want to catch the holy ghost and jump in your spirit."

Naomi flashes a smile. "Oh my. Ms. Shantae was right. You are very charming."

Devin waves his hand in the air and attracts the server's attention to the table. He orders enough drinks for everyone to relax and become acquainted.

Naomi raises her glass for a toast and yells, "to new beginnings!"

Everyone clings their glasses, chants to new beginnings, and consumes their drinks.

"Okay, Naomi. The floor is yours," Devin announces.

"Thank you. I promise my stories will make you self-reflect on your daily living.

"Imagine being an unwanted and unattractive high school girl. The guys would pass me by, and my confidence left with them—the art of rejection trails into adulthood.

"My coworkers were heavily involved in LS, and my team leader would always brag about her sex life. One day, her husband brought her lunch, and on his way out, he complimented my lips. The next thing I knew, I was involved in my first threesome.

"To make a long story short. I became the DTF for them and a few other couples.

"Shit was exciting at first. I went from being neglected to the chosen one at the parties. I began to dress better, learned to apply makeup, and style my hair. My confidence rose every time I created orgasms and happiness for the couples I fucked.

"I went from the shy girl to being the single arrogant bitch; choosing who I wanted to fuck, taking other women, men, and money. Of course, word got out, and they ousted me from the lifestyle."

"Sounds like a rag-to-riches movie," Vee hints.

"My mom would always tell me that everything that glitters isn't gold," Naomi mentions.

She lifts her dress and reveals keloid scars on her upper thighs, abdomen, and hips. "As I said before, I was exiled but not without some war wounds."

"Oh my God," Vee shouts.

She covers her mouth, slides out of her seat, and runs out of the restaurant.

Devin throws some dollars on the tables to cover the tab, apologizes to Naomi, and chases behind Vee.

He finds her trembling with her keys in her hand, too nervous to drive.

He approaches her carefully. "Vee, breathe. Forget about the assignment. Allow me to take you home and ensure you don't hurt yourself or do anything crazy."

He creeps closer and wraps her in his arms. He whispers in her ears, "it's okay. I got you."

She feels the warmth of his breath mixed with the comforting of his words and stops shaking. She slides from his hold and pushes him as hard as possible, screaming, "get away from me."

Being tipsy from the alcohol shifts his balance. He trips and falls on the concrete.

Vee unlocks her car, jumps in, and drives away.

Devin stares at the rear taillights as they disappear down the road. He dusts his clothes, cusses under his breath, and walks back into the establishment.

Naomi runs up. "Is everything okay? I'm sorry for the chaos I started."

"Don't worry about it. That bitch has been a looney toon since our first encounter. I can't believe I allowed her to get close to me. Fuck this sponsoring bullshit. That's one hoe that can survive on her own."

"You can't think that way. She's suffering and trying to adapt to change. Don't give up on her because she will need a sponsor."

"If you say so. By the way, there's one thing intriguing me about you. Why is a DTF or unicorn meeting people in a swinger establishment?"

"It's a safe place without judgment from the outside world. No pressure to fuck strangers. The food and music are the main attraction."

She smiles and points toward the guy in the Djay booth. "He's the real reason I'm here. That's my husband, and he accepted me when I was at my lowest point."

She hugs him. "Take care, Devin. And remember what I said."

Devin listens, but tonight is not about saving hoes. It's about reuniting with one.

He thanks Naomi for sharing her story and walks outside. He scrolls through his phone log and finds someone to make him erase the thoughts of Vee. He stops at the screen name 'Sophia the Squirter.'

"Oh, hell yeah. Time to open the floodgates!" he shouts.

He taps his Uber app and voyages off to his destination.

Chapter 14

Sophia curls her lips and shakes her head at Devin. "I know you didn't call and wake me from my sleep for a dead dick. You better pop a blue pill, slap the head, or let me suck it."

"Woman, you talk too much. Don't worry about Devastation; it always rises to the occasion," Devin assures. "I didn't pay you to suck or fuck. I want you to play in your pussy until it floods the sheets."

"Yes, daddy," she moans.

Devin admires the black and purple, floral-printed, cupless corset she is wearing. "I know you will taste delicious tonight," he compliments.

Sophia squirms in the sheets, licking her lips and touching herself.

He smiles as she removes the night bloom pasties and reveals two round brown areoles.

"Do you wanna taste them in your mouth, Daddy? Come here and let Mommy feed you," she teases.

He slides into the bed, rolls her on top of him, and stares into her eyes. "Kiss me," he commands.

He wraps his arms around her neck and forces her mouth open. Their tongues dance with each other's as they moan in unison for surrender. He runs his fingers through her hair and bites her neck.

She closes her eyes, exhales, and scrapes his chest with her nails. She kisses his chest in three different spots before returning her tongue to his mouth.

She grinds her body on top of him and takes a moment to slip one finger inside her drenched pussy. She pulls it out and wipes it across his lips. "Umm. Do you like that, Daddy?"

He rises from the bed, squeezes her titties, and she cries out for more. He kisses her belly button and trails his tongue along the center of her chest. She throws her head back as he massages her breasts and nipples.

"Sophia, do you like that?"

"Yes, Daddy! I love it."

He flicks his tongue over the left nipple and pinches the right nipple. He inhales and sucks the left breast into his mouth, taking turns biting and sucking.

Sophia grabs her left breast and places it in her mouth.

Devin watches as her greedy ass attempts to out-suck him, but he refuses to lose dominance.

DEVASTATION

He summons Devastation, and Sophia feels the hardness pressing against her clit.

He slurps and pulls his mouth from her nipples. The popping from his suction produces an echo throughout the room.

He stretches her nipple with his teeth, and she screams, "Ooh, Daddy, I love when you do that!"

"Have you been a good girl for Daddy?"

"Yes, Daddy. I have been on my best behavior."

"Who has been in my pussy since the last time I was here?"

"Nobody," she whines. "I would never disrespect your dick. My pussy only pulsates for you."

"That's my girl."

He wraps his hands around her waist and glides her pussy onto his face. She grabs the back of his head for leverage. He shakes his head, nose, and tongue while eating her pussy.

She rides his face, grips her nipples, and watches Devin's lips slap over her clit.

"Oh, baby, you're about to make me cum."

"Umm hmm," he moans.

He reaches his hands under her legs and latches them around her inner thighs. He takes two fingers and runs them over her clit.

She throws her head back and yells, "oh fuck!"

He runs his fingers deeper into her pussy, pulls them out, and jiggles them over her clit.

"Sophia, give me that nut," he demands.

She arches her back and pushes her hips over his face. "Are you ready for the Sophia Special?"

She reaches over the side of the bed, grabs her magic wand, and sets it to vibrate on her clit as Devin's tongue plows over her lips.

Devin enjoys the sensation of the wand tickling his nose as he sips her wetness.

She increases the wand speed, and Devin matches her momentum. She closes her mouth and anticipates her orgasm coming. She squirts, and Devin feels the warmness entering his mouth.

She gives him a second facial that splatters over his nose and runs down his cheeks.

Sophia jumps when she feels Devastation rising between her legs.

Devin reminds Sophia, "this muthafucka is not playing dead now."

"But you said we weren't fucking?"

"Plan changes. Spin your ass around and get on your knees."

He changes positions, strokes his dick, and glides Devastation into Sophia from behind. He slides his hands up her back until they grip her shoulders.

"Are you ready for Devastation?" he asks.

"Give it all to me," she begs.

He yanks her shoulders and strokes her deep at the same time.

"Oh shit!" she cries.

He twists his fingers in her hair and tugs her backward. He slams his dick into her pussy, creating the perfect clapping sound.

"Harder, Daddy," she moans.

He slaps her ass cheek, pushes her flat into the bed, and slowly grinds his dick from behind. "You love this dick. Tell me you love this dick."

"I love it, Daddy!"

He slides out, turns her around, and she wraps her legs around his lower back.

He stares into her eyes. "Squirt one more time, and I'll pay you extra."

She nods her head and embraces his inches. He lifts her legs higher, clinches his ass muscles, and delivers the devastating strokes she needs.

He slides his dick into warp speed mode and smashes through her pussy. She begs him to slow down, but he ignores her cries. He knows she wants pain, and he cannot stop until she squirts.

"Bitch, wet up the sheets. Wet these muthafuckers up."

She slides her hands over her clit as he pounds her pussy like cops knocking on the door, looking for a murder suspect.

"Devin. Devin. Devin," she moans.

He pulls out his dick and strokes it, waiting for the eruption from her pussy. She didn't disappoint and erupted like the Old Faithful Geyser of California.

The overflow went over the pillows, Devin's stomach, and the sheets.

"Hell yeah! That's why I fuck with you. No one can squirt like Sophia. You did that shit."

She runs her hands over her tits—"anything for you, Daddy. Devin, it's late. Why don't you stay and leave in the morning?"

Vee's meltdown is causing a ripple effect with his rules. He is willing to switch things up to clear his mind.

"I'll be right back," he informs.

He runs to the restroom and returns with the hair dryer.

Sophia gives him a strange look. "Where are you going with the hairdryer?"

"I paid for you to wet the sheets, not for me to sleep in them. This bed feels like an ocean."

Sophia sits and laughs while watching Devin air out the sheets and pillows. After 10 minutes of drying everything, he is finally ready to lie down.

He crawls into the bed and wraps his arms around her as Devastation pulsates against her ass cheeks.

He knows he will fuck her before the sun rises, but right now, he wants to sleep in peace, cuddling with a beautiful woman.

FLENARDO

DEVASTATION

Chapter 15

Joe Joe pounces on the bed, barks, and licks Vee's face until she rolls over. He jumps down to the floor, wags his tail, and barks relentlessly by the bedroom door.

Vee slips on her slippers and housecoat. "Okay, Joe Joe. Mama is coming."

She stands and stretches her arms over her head. She drops her arms and turns her torso from side to side to loosen her back.

She opens her mouth wide, yawns, and walks into the living room as Joe Joe follows behind her every step of the way.

She grabs the leash from the hook. "Up," she instructs while wiping her eyes.

Joe jumps on the couch and sits patiently while Vee connects the leash to his harness.

She walks outside and thinks about the pain Naomi endured in the lifestyle. Naomi's scars teleported Vee to her first boyfriend, Damien 'The Demon'.

He was one of the worst mistakes Vee made in her life. All it took was a sparkling smile, wicked tattoos, with a touch of hood arrogance.

Vee wished she had heeded her mother's warning. *"Veronica, a twenty-one-year-old man, has no business trying to date a sixteen-year-old high school girl,"* her mother would always say.

Of course, Vee was hot in the ass. She wasn't fucking, but she did suck the star quarterback's dick under the school bleachers.

Everyone is on *R. Kelly*, but in her high school days, it seems normal for a grown man to pick up or drop off young girls at high school.

Damien was the perfect gentleman at first. After high school, she left home and moved in with him. He became a wolf in sheep's clothing in less than two weeks.

"Vee, your ass better find a job or start selling pussy. All the gifts and money I gave you come with a price tag, and I'm cashing in."

Vee never forgot when the sick bastard tried forcing her to have an orgy with his homeboys. She refused and found a job at Winn Dixie to repay the money.

DEVASTATION

He would take her paycheck every Friday when she got paid. If he needed the money earlier, he would show up at the job and get it from her manager since they were friends.

Vee knew if she returned home, her mother would make her stand before the church and repent her sins.

Vee continued to work and suffered verbal and physical abuse. Damien would beat her with a belt during sex or choke her until she passed out.

She lived in hell for two years until she found the courage to leave while he was out of town for two weeks.

Luckily her father had a soft spot for his little girl and wired her some money. She gathered her belongings, caught a train, and moved in with some relatives out of state.

"Vee! Vee, get your fucking dog out of my grass," Michaels yells.

Vee has been walking and daydreaming about her past and never realizes Joe Joe was taking his morning shit in Michael's yard again.

Vee giggles and whispers, "good boy. You are getting two treats today."

She sticks her middle finger up in Michael's direction. "Tell your girl the truth, and I'll stop. Until then, fuck you!"

Joe Joe kicks up the grass with his hind legs and returns to Vee.

They walk back into the house, and Vee gives Joe his treats and searches for her phone.

There was no good morning text from Devin, and she was too proud to send one herself. She hopes she can salvage their friendship before he permanently cuts her off.

She decides to shower, slips on some clothes, and calls her best friend, Kaylene. "Girl, let's go thrift shopping."

"Vee, pick me up after two. I have another client's pussy to wax, and then I'll be free."

Kaylene has been Vee's best friend since they met at the waxing salon. They hang out from time to time, depending on their schedules.

Vee has a lot of free time since she doesn't work, but her inheritance will not last forever. She knows the million dollars would be handy, but her addiction is deeper than becoming a millionaire.

Surprisingly, she didn't drive home from the bar last night, drank herself into a coma or wake up with a stranger's dick in her mouth.

She hugs Joe and leaves her house. She drives to the park and reads until Kaylene finishes her last client. She has tons of books on her kindle.

DEVASTATION

Today she's reading *Blood Money* by J. Asmara.

She loves hood tales, and sometimes she uses books to distract her away from sex. It doesn't always work but it allows her to support a new author.

Once at the park, she inhales the fresh air and watches a man feeding bread to the ducks. She glances at the playground and admires the kids swinging and playing on the slide. *Such innocence and no worries about the world,* she thinks.

She watches a little girl run and jump in her dad's arms. She wishes her father was around to hug her. To tell her things will be okay and that he will protect her from all her pain and misery.

A text pings on Vee's phone. It's an alert from the Facebook Dating app. She has been talking to a guy name Marquis for several weeks.

He texts that he would like to meet tonight if she's free. She informs him to plan the date and send the meet-up location.

He sends a smiley face, and she returns a cross-fingers emoji. She never has luck with dating apps, but maybe tonight could be a new opportunity.

She's convinced guys want to fuck and date but not commit to a relationship. Maybe it's her personality, or they can smell the numerous dicks seeping from her pores.

She feels herself making strides, and it has been a week since she's fucked or sucked. Abstaining for a week is a lifetime on a nympho planet, and she pats herself on the back.

She taps her iPad, returns to the previous chapter, and reads until Kaylene calls.

Time passes, and she finishes the book. "Another one down," she congratulates herself.

She stares at the time and pulls out her phone. It rings, and she answers, "Bitch, it's about time!"

"I'm sorry. The last woman's pussy looked like Chewbacca. It took forever to wax," she jokes.

"Girl, your ass is crazy. I'm on my way to pick you up."

"Outstanding! I'll be waiting."

Vee closes her iPad, packs her things, and walks to the truck.

She finds some music to listen to before leaving the parking lot. Today is *Bon Jovi's Living 'on a Prayer*.

Tommy used to work on the docks.

Union been on strike.

DEVASTATION

He's down on his luck. It's tough.

So tough...

She catches the chorus and sings,

We've gotta hold on to what we've got.

It doesn't make a difference if we make it or not.

We've got each other and that's a lot for love.

We'll give it a shot!

Whoa. We're halfway there.

Whoa. Livin' on a prayer.

Take my hand. We'll make it, I swear.

Whoa. Livin' on a prayer.

She flips down her sunglasses, opens her sunroof, and sings all the way to Kaylene's job.

FLENARDO

Chapter 16

Vee honks her horn. "Get in, bitch. Everyone will buy all the good shit if we don't hurry."

Kaylene gets in and fastens her seat belt. "Okay, Veronica Marie Hemsley. I'm ready."

"Wow, we're using full government names now?" Vee responds.

Vee proceeds to drive to Found by the Pound. It's a hip, funky, bohemian thrift store in South St. Louis.

They park the car and walk through the parking lot. A homeless man approaches them with a sign reading, 'I'll work for food.'

Vee wonders what her future would be like if she ran out of money. Will she hold a sign with the phrase 'I'll fuck for food'?

She tips the man a few dollars, and the man says, "God bless you."

Kaylene asks the homeless man, "have you heard about a homeless guy flashing his penis to people?"

He stares at them without saying a word, presses his index finger over his lips, and tells them to "shh." He looks over his shoulder to make sure no one is watching.

He extends his hand, saying, "I can tell you where he sleeps for ten dollars."

Kaylene smiles and tells Vee to pay the man his money.

"You are the one excited about a penis scavenger hunt. You pay for the sausage party," Vee jokes.

Kaylene gives the man ten dollars. "Okay, where is the penis bandit?"

He glances around and waves them to come closer in his direction. He slides his shorts a few inches down his hips and pulls out the meatiest chocolate wrinkle dick they've ever seen.

"Here you go, ladies. I'm the flasher." He jerks a patch of knotted pubic hair out and blows it toward their faces. He shakes his dick while walking towards them.

Vee and Kaylene sprint through the parking lot as the homeless man chases behind them.

They scream and run toward the store. They reach the front of the entrance and stop to catch their breath.

They turn around and see the homeless guy laughing while peeping behind a car.

"What the fuck, Kaylene?"

DEVASTATION

"Veronica Marie, calm down."

Kaylene places her hand over her heart. "Damn, I haven't run that fast since high school. I overheard some women at the salon talking about a homeless guy flashing people with a twelve-inch sausage. We've seen a real-life Bigfoot with balls!"

"Girl, he did have a big dick," Vee compliments.

"Yeah. Thick, stinky, and dirty," Kaylene responds.

"Okay, enough talking about Dirty Dick Dan. Let's find this vintage vanity before someone buys it," Vee said.

They stroll to the furniture department, and Vee claps her hands and smiles as she notices the vanity is still available.

The vintage 1930s vanity has seven drawers, three on either side and one curved drawer in the center—original caster wheels, wood grain, and the tiara-style mirror.

A cheerful customer service rep comes and assists them with the vanity. "Ms. Hemsley, I presume."

"Yes, that's me."

"Nice to meet you. We can deliver the vanity in three days if you are ready to complete the purchase."

"What's the story behind the mirrors? Has anyone died while applying makeup?" Kaylene questions.

"No, I think the vanity is harmless," the service rep assures.

Kaylene smacks her lips and says, "yeah, right. Have you ever seen the movie about the handicapped man who befriended his reflection, and the demon in the mirror made him kill everyone he loved? This mirror looks just like the one in the movie."

"I could use a demon in the mirror late at night. Maybe it would eat my pussy when I'm lonely," Vee jokes.

Kaylene and Vee laugh, making the customer service rep crack his serious expression.

"Okay. Run my debit card, and I'll sign the paperwork for the delivery," Vee states.

Vee leaves the store with a pep in her step. She can't wait to add her unique enhancements to the vanity.

She turns to Kaylene as they approach the car. "Do you think Dirty Dick Dan is lurking around the parking lot?"

"Girl, I love that nickname. I can't wait to tell everyone at the salon about today's adventure."

Vee chuckles and presses the key fob to unlock the door. "Are you ready for Starbucks?"

"A Caramel Ribbon Crunch Frappe and a birthday cake pop sounds like the perfect way to close the evening," Kaylene adds.

DEVASTATION

Vee drives through the city while Kaylene places their orders from the app. They arrive, grab the bag, and pull out the birthday cake pops.

They tap the pops together. "Cheers to thrift shopping and getting flashed by a stinky dick!"

They sing and dance in the car while traveling to Kaylene's house. Vee parks the vehicle, jumps out, and runs around the truck to give Kaylene the tightest hug ever. "Thanks for hanging out with me. I miss these moments. Hopefully, we can plan another one soon."

"I'll be waiting and be safe tonight," Kaylene responds.

"You know I will. I'll call you with an update after the date ends," Vee assures.

Vee watches Kaylene enter her home before leaving to prepare for her date with Marquis.

She unlocks her front door, pats Joe on the head, and rushes into the bathroom. She takes a shower, washes her hair, and shaves her legs.

She wears her hair straight for the evening and slips on a black and gray Calvin Klein T-Shirt Dress. She tops the outfit off with her low-cut black chucks, glittery silver tongue, white laces, skull necklace, bracelet, and earrings set.

She takes a selfie in the mirror and sends the picture to Marquis with the caption, *this is what I'm wearing.*

He replies, *ok, I'll come casually as well.*

"Joe Joe, your Mommy has a date tonight. You better be a good boy while I'm gone."

Joe Joe barks, reminding Vee to give him his favorite treat before she walks out the door.

She tosses Joe his treat and grabs her keys and purse. She checks her phone, praying Devin will send a text to see if she's okay.

She feels neglected but brushes it off with the thoughts of a delicious dinner and a possible one-night stand.

She enters the address for Joey B's on the Hill in her GPS, checks her makeup, and drives away.

She tells Marquis she loves Italian, and he promises this spot is perfect for her tastebuds.

She arrives early, enters the restaurant, and requests a booth table. She sits, pulls the phone out of her purse, and text Marquis.

He responds he is running late but will be there shortly.

Strike one, she thinks to herself.

She orders a drink and reads on her iPad until the server or Marquis shows up first. Of course, it was the server, and she wasted no time sipping her drink.

DEVASTATION

She reads five chapters, pauses for a break, and checks the time. *I can't believe this man is thirty minutes late.*

She texts him again. *Don't bother showing up if you are not here in five minutes. This is truly annoying and disrespectful to keep a woman waiting this long.*

She can see the screen blinking with his response. *I'm pulling into the parking lot right now.*

She exhales and mumbles "whatever" under her breath.

Marquis enters the restaurant wearing a durag, gym shorts, a dirty white wife-beater, socks, and slides.

He approaches the table, smiles, and greets Vee. "Sorry for keeping you waiting. I didn't have time to grab my clothes from the cleaners."

"Who clothes are you wearing on your Facebook page? I feel like I'm on an episode of catfish."

"No worries, Vee. It's me." He stretches out his arm, revealing the angel wing tattoo with the picture of his mother underneath.

"I'm glad we didn't go anywhere too fancy," Vee said.

"Can a brotha catch a break? I'll make it up to you on the second date."

"Shit! We might not even finish the first," she hints.

He smiles and winks at Vee. "You look lovely tonight."

"Thanks. You look like you are coming from a pickup basketball game. Marquis, I'm going to be honest with you. There will not be a second date. I'm going to block you before I get to my car."

"Wait, Vee. Please allow me to make things right. What can I do to turn this situation around?"

He licks his lips and brushes his hands over his shorts.

Vee notices his dick print and smiles.

"Okay, Marquis. There is something I would like for you to do. If you do it correctly, you might get another date."

"Sure. I'm down," he said.

"Have you ever eaten pussy from the back in a car? I'm parked outside, and I could use a quick nut. I'm not fucking you, but I want to bust my juices on your face."

"Say less," he said.

They walk outside, and she folds her back seat, props up on her knees, and lifts her ass in the air. Marquis kneels behind her, raises her skirt, slides her panties to the side, and sucks on her clit.

She jerks and throws her ass over his face. "Eat this pussy. Make me cum for being late."

She will block him on the app once she gets home, but she can get a nut and write the entry in her diary.

DEVASTATION

Chapter 17

Devin paces from the living room to the kitchen, wondering if he should call Vee for their Criminal Minds ritual.

He looks at the phone and tosses it back down. Vee is the one that should call and apologize. With her fucked up attitude. Days like these are why he buys pussy and keeps his feelings away from women.

He jumps on the sofa, grabs the remote, and searches for his favorite series. Today's episode is called *The Boogeyman*. The plot speaks about the team traveling to a small town to investigate children's murders.

This episode sounds like a great thriller.

He enjoys the first five minutes but misses the scent of Vee's perfume lingering under his nose as she lies on his chest and plays with his locs.

I'm not interested in the pussy and this bitch has me missing her crazy ass.

He grabs his phone and dials her number. She answers excitedly but quickly changes her voice to sound nonchalant.

"Listen, Vee. I'm not here to argue or speak about you being possessed in the parking lot that night. Criminal Minds is on, and I am missing my mystery-solving partner."

"Devin, I wanted to text you countless times, but I feared you would cuss me out for pushing you to the ground and speeding off into the night."

"Naomi asked me not to give up on you. Plus, watching this series alone is boring. Stop overanalyzing everything and bring your ass over to my penthouse."

"I'll be there in five minutes."

"What the hell? Your stalkerish ass is probably around the corner."

"Yes. I'm at the store near your neighborhood. I have been here for an hour, practicing how I could apologize for another stupid mistake."

"Vee, every day we are going to do something stupid. There's no need to practice anymore. Just tell me when you arrive," he jokes. "Give the security guard one of my favorite Stephen King quotes."

"Sometimes human places create inhuman monsters," Vee yells over the phone.

"How the hell did you know I would say that?"

DEVASTATION

Vee chuckles over the phone. "We are whores, and psychotic friends united to win a million dollars."

"Touché," Devin responds.

"I'm heading to the kitchen to fix a delicious bowl of cookies and cream. I'll throw a cherry on top as a truce. No more fighting, and let's get this money," he announces.

They disconnect the call, and he walks into the kitchen and opens the freezer door.

He places the Blue Bunny carton on the counter and grabs a large bowl from the cabinet.

After their last few dates, he memorizes Vee's love for gothic and skulls. He ordered and engraved a set of stainless-steel spoons with the words 'you have been poison' with crossbones and a skull at the bottom.

He cannot wait to see the priceless reaction on her face once he surprises her with the spoons.

He grabs his heavy-duty ice cream scooper and dips it in the carton. He rolls a giant ball and dumps it in the bowl. He repeats the process until the ice cream scoops are higher than the bowl and some creams flow out of the bowl.

He uses his finger and wipes it up. Without hesitation, he sticks his fingers in his mouth and sucks off the cream.

He dims the lights, places the bowl on the coffee table, and waits for Vee to knock on the door.

He hears two soft knocks on the door, followed by a pause and another two knocks.

His heart flutters, and he flashes a smile before opening the door. He takes a bow and gestures his welcoming hand into his home. "I scream, you scream, we all scream for ice cream."

"Devin, you are so corny. Get out of the way." She pushes him to the side, kicks off her shoes at the door, and walks to the sofa.

"Yes, my favorite!" she shouts. She grabs the bowl of ice cream and bites the cherry. She dips the spoon, pulls out a glob of ice cream, slurps it clean, and notices the engravement.

She reads the words with her lips and smiles at Devin, who is still standing by the door watching her loving the surprise.

"You didn't see that coming, did you?" he asked.

"Not at all. You know men don't do anything nice for me. Soooo… are you going to let me put some ice cream on your dick and slurp it like this?"

She dips her spoon in for another scoop of ice cream, opens her mouth wide, and places it in her mouth. She demonstrates gagging over the spoon before yanking it out.

She laughs and tells Devin, "this could be us, but you don't like free pussy."

"Yes, you're right. And you don't care for dick unless you are drunk. Now be a nice girl, and let's watch Criminal Minds."

He sits down, presses play, and eats some ice cream before Vee eats the entire bowl.

Ten minutes into the series, Vee asks Devin which detective he would pay to fuck.

"Umm. Give me a second to answer that one. There are not many attractive main characters on the show," he answers.

"There isn't one attractive guy in your house either because I can't get lucky."

He continues to watch the show and chooses Penelope a few minutes later.

"What the fuck? Are you serious?" Vee asks.

"You have a better selection with the men; I know you would suck the soul out of Derek."

He grabs the remote and switches to CSI Miami. "Now, this is where all the hot bitches live. I'd fuck Calleigh, Alexx, Yelina, Maria, and Horatio's ex-wife, the saved-by-the-bell chick," he proclaims.

"Thirsty ass. I'm sure you'll empty your bank account fucking with them."

"My fuck account is like my strokes…Deep."

"That's the shit I like to hear. Keep on talking shit. You're getting my pussy wet.

"Devin, I don't have anything planned tonight. I've never seen or heard about someone buying pussy. Do you think I could watch you order some?"

"Ordering pussy isn't like ordering grub hub, Vee." he laughs. But he never turns down a chance to be adventurous. "Okay, let's finish this episode of Criminal Minds, and I'll think of someone that loves dick and pussy."

"Sound like my type of evening, and I can't wait to see this shit." She sang a verse from the song Bills Paid, "Keep the pussy juicy like it's marinated (Uh) The way I be killin' shit, I need interro'gatin (Woo)."

"Vee, what do you know about Latto and City Girls?"

"What? Have you lost your mind? This pussy is from the sunshine state. I peel this bitch back sweeter than oranges."

"I knew Malakai should have given me a better sponsor. Your ass is nothing but trouble."

She giggles and snuggles next to him. "Okay, I'll relax and finish this episode. I promised no more sex talk until tonight."

"Agreed. Now, let's solve this crime," Devin suggests.

FLENARDO

DEVASTATION

Chapter 18

Vee stands in awe of Devin's creative space for working and searching for pussy. She looks through the skylight windows and counts the stars.

He has the perfect view of Downtown St. Louis, and she is envious of Devin for being able to see this magical moment every night.

She leans closer and notices the apartment window directly across from them is clear without a curtain or blinds.

As soon as she tilts closer, a voluptuous woman with blonde hair leads a man into the bedroom. The woman drops to her knees, pull down the gentlemen's pants, and performs oral sex.

Vee watches as the man yanks her hair and drives his dick in her mouth. Vee steps away from the windows once she feels wetness sliding into her thong.

She plays it off and turns to Devin. "I was jealous of the view, but now I'm pissed. You have live porn, and you aren't interested in watching them fuck."

He smiles and powers on his laptop. "That's the Henderson's. They moved in about a month ago. She sucks his dick every night at nine-thirty. The first couple of nights, I masturbated, but it has become the norm for me.

"On Friday mornings, I guess it's Mrs. Henderson's time to receive her orgasm. She wakes up, turns over, and straddles his face."

"Next Thursday, I'm staying the night," Vee said.

"Bring your pepping ass over here, and let's purchase some pussy for tonight."

Devin clicks some keys, and numbers and letters flood the screen like in the Matrix movie. After about thirty seconds, the screens turn black, flash twice, and the words Cunnilingus Corner emerge.

"What the hell are you into?" Vee asks.

"You heard of the dark web? This is the deepest corner of Earth. Only the elite can access this site, and everyone's sensitive information is sealed and never breached."

"How can I become a member?" Vee inquires.

"You can't," Devin responds. "You know you are too messy for this profession, plus you aren't trying to spend money to get dicked down. I'll choose. Look out the window or something."

"Well, hurry up and choose someone so I can ask how much money you are about to spend."

Devin types an encrypted password, and a message appears on the screen, *What are your desires, Mr. Williams?*

He stares at the wall, wiggles his fingers over the keyboard, and yells, "Got it."

He types again, and Vee looks over his shoulder. "I want to know what you got. Is that all you have to do? I was expecting more from buying pussy."

"You have no idea what we are about to do. I have many outlets for buying pussy, but nothing beats The Corner when I'm adventurous."

He closes the site, powers down the PC, and jumps from the seat. "Come on; we have places to be and people to eat."

He walks to a safe, spins the combination, and retrieves a black phone.

He turns around, "Vee, leave all your identifications here, and don't bring your phone."

"What if there's an emergency?"

"Vee, shut up for once before I decide to send you home and enjoy this ride alone. Now bring your ass on," he demands.

They leave the penthouse and ride the elevator down to the main lobby. They walk by the night shift guard, and he throws his hand in the air and informs them to be safe.

Once outside, Devin pulls the phone from his pants and texts a message. Moments later, a message returns, and Devin's face glows under the night sky.

"Why are you so cheery, and should I ask the valet for my car?"

"Nope. No car. We are walking, and the destination is only seventeen minutes from here."

"I didn't bring the right shoes."

"No worries. When you are tired, you can ride on my back."

"Oh, a bitch can ride on your back but not your dick? Only Devin Williams can reject my good pussy."

They walk down the sidewalk, take a left at the corner, and cross over to Market Street. Devin has long legs and remembers to take shorter strides so Vee can keep up.

Without thinking, he slips his fingers inside Vee's hand, and she ignores the affection and attention. She didn't want to ruin the moment or make Devin cuss her out before they reached their destination.

DEVASTATION

She would steal glances at Devin as they walked. Admiring his creative loc hairstyle, muscular physique, and of course, the way his dick swings with every step

It reminds her of an old clock swinging from side to side at her grandmother's house.

Yeah, bitch, don't fuck this moment up, she thinks.

They arrive at Union Station, and there's no one else around. She thinks Devin is full of shit but allows the night to continue playing out.

They approach the locked entrance. Devin scans his phone over the pad, and the gate opens.

They walk through the park and stop in front of the two-hundred-foot St. Louis Wheel.

"What the fuck, Devin? I hope you didn't bring me here to ride a Ferris Wheel."

He snickers and winks his eye. He opens the gondola door. "Step inside for the ride of your life."

Vee steps inside, and in the corner of the gondola is a six-foot reddish buzz low haircut Swedish woman with dimples.

Vee stares at her blue jeans shorts, revealing her booty cheeks, black boots, and a long sleeve crop shirt.

Vee assumes they are here for a threesome. She claps her hands together and drops to her knees. "God, I knew you were real."

"Get your crazy ass up. I'm going to leave you ladies alone and start the Ferris wheel," Devin mentions.

"Wait, you aren't staying?" Vee asks.

"No, this sale is all you. Quit talking. You only have three or four rotations in the air. Time is ticking."

He closes the door and walks over and starts the wheel.

Vee stares and is hypnotized by the Swedish woman's blue eyes and tattoos.

The gondola shakes, lifts, and circles through the night sky. Vee has never been on a Ferris Wheel before. She feels nauseous and hopes she doesn't vomit on the woman.

The woman slides her hand over Vee's thigh. "Relax, darling. I will take care of you. My name is Magna, which means a mighty strong woman."

Vee shrinks in her seat. "Yes, I can tell you are strong. You are almost taller than Devin."

She smiles and mentions the first circle is complete. "Devin requested that I make you cum before the wheel stops."

DEVASTATION

Without permission, Magna walks over and slides her tongue in Vee's mouth. She licks her lips and whispers in her ear, "damn, you taste good."

"Arch your back," Magna instructs.

Vee arches as Magna slides Vee's shorts and thongs to the floor.

Magna moans, slurps, and slowly circles her tongue over Vee's clit. Vee takes two fingers and stretches her pussy lips wider for more access.

"Ahh, Ahh," Vee moans as the Ferris Wheel spins around in the air.

Magna gulps gradually and retracts until her top lip is the only thing resting on Vee's clit. She returns with a little side-to-side lick.

She laps her tongue recklessly over Vee's lips, gripping her thighs and shaking her head while eating. She hovers her mouth over Vee's pussy, tugs, and nibbles the clit with her teeth.

Vee's clit swells and Magna sinks her teeth deeper as Vee cries a pleasurable "umm, umm."

"Ahh," Magna exhales.

She uses her tongue and slaps Vee's clit like a ping-pong ball going back and forth across the table.

Magna closes her eyes and spins her tongue faster. Vee arches her back higher, moans louder, and grabs her hair,

"Oh shit!" Vee screams.

Magna wobbles her head harder; tongue flicks increase with every lick.

Magna inserts two fingers and glides them deeper into Vee's pussy. She folds Vee's legs behind her head, finger fucking her pussy and slurping on her clit.

Vee shifts positions on the gondola floor and waves Magna over to finish the job.

Magna buries her face in Vee's pussy, and munches viciously. Vee grabs the back of Magna's head, forcing her face between her thighs and thrusting her pelvis simultaneously.

Magna licks swiftly and precisely over Vee's clit.

Vee's heart races inside her chest, her body trembles, and within seconds, she cums.

Magna refuses to let go, and Vee screams and tries to push her face away. Magna licks harder, and Vee cums repeatedly.

Vee's head spins more than the Ferris Wheel, and she is perplexed by the orgasm and being suspended in the air.

Magna retreats from Vee's thighs and blows her a kiss. "I could eat you all night. I knew your pussy would be delightful when you entered the gondola."

The wheels spin around and halt. Vee shakes her head and looks around. "What the fuck. I'm going to kill Devin."

The door opens, and Vee scrambles to find her clothes.

Devin smiles. "Magna, how many did she bust?"

"I lost count, but if you need my services again, don't hesitate to call." Magna steps over Vee and walks out of the gondola.

Devin reaches for Vee's hand. She slaps it away. "Go to hell, Devin. Never again will I ask about Cunnilingus Corner."

"Poor baby. Come on, you know you love Magna. I bet her tongue was long and thick."

"Fuck you, Devin!"

"Yeah, I know you want to. But you're not my type. Now get your ass up, and let's find a breakfast spot. You can tell me about the Magna Experience over steak and eggs."

Vee enjoyed having her pussy eaten as the wheel turned, but she didn't want to boast in front of Devin. She plays it off and can't wait to go home in the morning to write about this night in her diary.

Nympho Log is blowing up, she thinks.

Her head stopped spinning, and she wondered how Devin could secure the park and work the Ferris Wheel.

She shrugs her shoulders, slides on her shorts, and takes Devin's offer for breakfast.

Chapter 19

The six o'clock alarm buzzes, alerting Vee that it's time to get up and start her day. She yawns, and with her eyes still close, she mumbles, "The Henderson's."

She purposefully asked Devin if she could stay overnight to watch the morning show.

She snatches her phone, turns off the alarm, and tosses the cover to the left side of the bed. She yawns and stretches her arms over her head. She jumps up, runs to the bathroom, takes a morning piss, and washes her face.

She hums while brushing her teeth, rinses, and giggles at her reflection in the mirror. "Damn girl, you look like shit."

She brushes her hair, pulls it into a ponytail, and races toward Devin's office suite. Devin went to work and left her alone in the penthouse. She feels like a kid waiting on Santa to deliver Christmas gifts.

Her phone rings, and she answers in an impolite tone. "Hello, make it quick."

"Woman, calm your ass down. I checked the time and knew you were looking out my office window. There are some binoculars in the middle drawer."

"Oh shit! I can see Mrs. Henderson's face up close and personal."

"Make sure you mop your dripping pussy juices off my floor."

"How did you know my pussy drips?"

"Bye, Vee. Get off my damn phone."

She shrugs her shoulders, retrieves the binoculars, and waits for the Henderson's sex scene premiere.

She leans closer to the window and notices the bedroom is too large. "Oh no, my eyes are bigger than my orgasm. Let me back away a few feet."

She places the binoculars on the desk, slips her T-shirt over her head, and slides her panties down. Her right ankle tangles in the panties, preventing them from falling to the floor. She shakes her leg in the air and wiggles them to the ground.

"Whew, pulling my panties off was a workout. Finally, a bitch can watch neighborly porn freely and in peace."

She grabs the binoculars and notices Mrs. Henderson is no longer in bed with her husband.

DEVASTATION

Vee scans the bedroom. "Damn, did this bitch vanish in thin air? I know she didn't cum that fast. It only took me a moment to take my clothes off."

She wiped the binocular lens to ensure the image wasn't playing tricks on her mind. She adjusts her position, looks through the window, and sees the bathroom door open.

Mrs. Henderson steps into the bedroom wearing a sexy Supergirl cosplay costume. Vee zooms in on the blue velvet halter-top shirt that cuts off right under her rib cages.

Vee notices Mrs. Henderson's perky nipples. She licks her lips and admires the rest of the outfit.

She lowers the binoculars to Mrs. Henderson's perfect waistline and crystal navel piercing.

Vee squeezed her thighs together to slow down the wetness and was tempted to stop looking but wanted more.

Mrs. Henderson fans the ruffles of her blue miniskirt in the air. She dons a pair of red boots with heels that stop two inches over her calf muscles. She balls her fists and places them on the side of her hips.

She stands there, waiting to fight against the world's greatest supervillains.

She runs and dives in the air with her fist balled tightly in front of her like she's flying. She lands on the bed and bounces up with quickness.

"Go, Mrs. Henderson! Bitch is flying faster than the speed of light. Now, if this woman can blow cum out her mouth and it freezes, I'm running next door to get my pussy sucked."

Mrs. Henderson straddles and flips her skirt over Mr. Henderson's face.

Mrs. Henderson rides her waist upward and rotates it in a slow circle. She pulls the Supergirl's halter top over her head and rides his face, beating her fists against the headboard.

Mrs. Henderson flips around and rides his face in a reverse cowgirl method. She reaches her hand inside Mr. Henderson's underwear and pulls out his dick.

"Oh, this shit is fuckin' hot!" Vee shouts to herself.

Mrs. Henderson leans back and props one foot up on her tippy toe while riding his face. She takes two fingers, spreads her pussy lips wider, and fucks his face.

Vee sticks two fingers in her pussy, slides them out, and sucks the juices off them. She is getting hornier as she watches Mrs. Henderson getting ready to catch a morning nut.

Mr. Henderson flips Mrs. Henderson on her back. Mrs. Henderson clamps her ankles around his neck and thrusts her hips up. He latches his hands around her waist and forces her to feed him more.

Mrs. Henderson's body shivers, and she releases her ankle lock and starts to beat Mr. Henderson's back with her foot.

Mrs. Henderson rolls the back of her husband's head around her pussy like she is waxing cars.

She arches her back and smears her pussy into his face deeper.

Vee slips her fingers into herself again. She slides them out and jabs them back into her sopping-wet pussy relentlessly. Her pussy creams and she screams, "I need to get fucked!"

She throws the binoculars to the floor and snatches one of Devin's oversized T-shirts, a pair of socks, and her tennis shoes.

She hurries out of the office suite, runs down the stairs, and out the penthouse door. She sprints to the elevator and presses the lobby button multiple times before the doors open.

She leans against the elevator's corner to catch her breath. She presses the close-door button and rides to the main lobby.

She exits the elevator and sprints toward the security guard's desk. "Tell Devin I'll be back soon," she informs the guard as she runs faster out of the building.

She leaps down the steps and runs into the street. Her mind was focused on the Henderson's, she never looked left or right before crossing the street.

A bicyclist's attempts to brake were unsuccessful. He collides with Vee and knocks her to the ground. She tumbles, rolls, and springs up from the concrete.

"Woman, I almost killed your ass!"

"I'm sorry, boo. I'm ok if you're ok."

She keeps running toward the building and stops inside at the front desk. "Ma'am, can you please buzz the Henderson's floor? They are expecting me."

The lady notices Vee's scraped knees and elbows. "Do you need a band-aid or some alcohol?"

"No, I'm fine. Just call the penthouse."

The lady calls the apartment. "Mrs. Henderson, a woman with bloody knees, is here requesting to speak with you."

DEVASTATION

Vee snatches the phone from the woman. "Mrs. Henderson, I saw you in your super girl outfit and want to join the Justice League."

Vee was instructed to give the phone back to the security woman.

The woman takes the phone and responds to Mrs. Henderson. "You might have to give her crazy ass a band-aid."

The security woman hangs up the phone and smiles at Vee. "I have seen a lot of crazy shit in this building, but you are the craziest. You are cleared to go. They are on the top floor."

"Yeah, I know," she responds while rushing towards more elevators. She is bleeding and is short of breath but is adamant about joining the Henderson's morning routine.

She peeps her head out the elevator door, looks right, and sees Mrs. Henderson waving.

"I was wondering why you didn't come sooner. We saw you in the window. Get in here and clean your wounds in the bathroom before joining us."

Vee walks in and freezes in place from seeing Mr. Henderson stroking his dick.

"Baby, his Viagra isn't always strong. You better hurry before your trip is for nothing."

Vee hurries to the bathroom, finds the first aid kit, and bandages her wounds.

She exits the bathroom and joins the league. She gets on her knees and allows Mr. Henderson to fuck her from behind while she munches on his wife's pussy.

She grins and slobs on Mrs. Henderson's clit. *Nympho logs stories are becoming more breathtaking every day,* she thinks and continues to eat Mrs. Henderson's scrumptious pussy.

Mr. Henderson thrusts faster and knocks Vee's face deeper into Mrs. Henderson's pussy.

"You love watching us. Now feel this dick sliding through your walls. I'll teach your peeping Tom ass," Mr. Henderson utters.

Vee raises her face from Ms. Henderson's drizzling lips. "Yes, I'm a dirty whore that loves watching. Teach me, Mr. Henderson. Teach me," she pleads.

Mrs. Henderson pulls Vee's hair and returns her face between her thighs.

Mrs. Henderson looks up and smiles at her husband. "Thank God it's Friday."

They give each other a high five and enjoy the morning get-together.

DEVASTATION

Chapter 20

Devin was moments away from signing out of his computer until an email from Ms. Yu-Yan popped up. He clicks the side of his mouse, scrolls through the email, and opens the message.

Attached to the email were photos of his new condominium with an astonishing view of downtown Beijing.

In the photos is an oversized bedroom with a plush king-sized bed, an adjoining spa-inspired bathroom, and a deep-soaking tub with a built-in flat-screen TV over the tub.

He clicks the third picture and sees his elegant living room with a spacious kitchen.

He smiles, and a piece of him wants to respond yes to her offer, but he's nervous about being in a foreign country.

Another email pops in from Ms. Yu-Yan. *Wow, more surprises,* he thinks.

He opens it and sees photos of his gym containing free weights, a cable machine, and a Peloton bike and treadmill.

He scrolls to the last attachment with the caption, 'the best gift of them all.'

He clicks the attachment and watches a video of a five-foot-three Chinese woman sitting outside on the balcony with long, dark hair down to her butt.

She's wearing a black and white ruffled maid outfit that consists of a mini black dress, apron, and a cute hat. She's holding a sign with the words, 'Welcome Home, Devin.'

She drops the sign on the ground and holds up the international index finger for Devin to wait for a second. She pulls another maid in the video as well.

"We are here to ensure that you enjoy the best of Beijing during the day and night!" they proclaim.

They wave bye before the video ends.

Devin leans back in his chair, runs his fingers through his locs, and stares at the ceiling.

Day and Night? I can do some freaky shit with these ladies.

His phone rings and cuts into his fantasizing.

He answers the phone, and it's Mr. Gray, the security guard from his building.

"Good afternoon, Mr. Williams. Ms. Hemsley has locked herself out of the penthouse. Should I allow her to enter the penthouse or wait for you to return in the lobby?"

Devin could hear Vee shouting in the background about how she had left her ID and keys upstairs.

"Mr. Gray, please allow her upstairs before she causes a scene in the lobby."

"Yessir, Mr. Williams."

He ends the call, checks his alarm system, and waits for Vee to enter the penthouse.

The doors open, and Vee steps in wearing his Puma T-shirt that goes down to her lower thighs.

"Why is this lunatic wearing band-aids on her knees?"

He gathers his things, locks his office door, speaks to a few colleagues, and exits the building.

His phone rings again, and he assumes it's Vee. He answers without looking. "What the hell is your crazy ass doing now?"

"Excuse me? Did I call at the wrong time?"

He responds with a soft laugh before responding. "No, beautiful, not at all. I thought you were someone else."

"Damn, you are replacing me already?"

"Hard to erase my first impression of seeing you and all the memories we created."

"Glad to hear that I'm still on your mind. Do you have time to meet up later?"

"Armocita, I'll make time for you."

"Wonderful! I'm about to jump in the shower. I'll text you my address and see you soon."

He flashes back to the time when they fucked on his Peloton bike. His dick begins to swell, and he adjusts his pants to keep his erection tamed momentarily.

"Armocita or Ms. Cupcake? Today, I'm feeling extra nasty and ready to taste your Little Debbie."

He receives her address and types it into the Uber app—only a twenty-minute ride. That is outstanding, and I can chat with Vee's crazy ass during the drive.

The Uber app notified him the car was ten minutes away. He switches screens and calls Vee.

"Veronica, Veronica, Veronica. You should have grabbed your keys before rushing out the door. Did you have a wonderful time with the Henderson's?"

"How the hell did you know I went over there?"

"Mr. Gray mentioned you ran across the street without looking and were hit by a bicyclist. I figured the sex demon inside of you was thirsty."

She laughs before answering, "the demon released all over Mr. Henderson's dick."

"Vee, your ass is too wild for me. I won't be home tonight, but you are welcome to stay, and I'll see you in the morning."

DEVASTATION

"After the morning I had. I think I'm going to shower and take a nap. Talk to you later."

Devin ends the call as the Uber driver pulls alongside the curb. He verifies the driver's tag, opens the door, and slides into the back seat.

He closes his eyes during the ride and thinks of all the crazy shit he wants to do with Armocita. He can't wait to inhale her perfume, bite her neck, and trails his tongue over her sexy tattoo.

The driver pulls up to the address. "Mr. Williams, we are here."

"Damn, that was fast. Enjoy your five stars and tip."

He gathers his things from the car and walks toward Armocita's apartment.

Armocita lives on the third floor, and Devin takes his time climbing the steps. He figures she could use a few more minutes to prepare for their afternoon.

He reaches the last steps, turns left, and looks around for apartment 313.

He followed the odd numbers on the apartment doors until he stopped in front of hers. The door opens, and her arm appears from behind the door. Devin immediately glances at her soft hand with colorful manicure nails waving for him to enter.

He walks in without looking back as he approaches her living room.

"Turn around, Mr. Williams."

Devin's eyes widen as he stares at Armocita's naked, lean, and toned body. Her pussy, was freshly shaved, and her abs begged him to lick them. Her makeup was flawless, with a touch of purple lipstick.

She spins around, and he appreciates the three-sixty view. She lifts her right leg with her ankle and folds it behind her head. She balances everything like a stork in the pond.

Devin sees the wetness dripping from her thick and dark pussy lips.

She returns her legs to the ground, walks to the living room, pushes him on the sofa, and sits on his lap. "Devin, do you know what I desire?"

He inhales her perfume. "No, baby. Please tell me, and I'll fulfill it. But I can't do anything unless you ask me to pay for your services first."

"How rude of me. Allow me to try again. Devin, it's two hundred and fifty for you to eat my ass. Five hundred if you replace your tongue with your dick."

"Now we are speaking my language," he expresses.

DEVASTATION

He lifts her from his lap and onto her knees. He leans his head near her asshole and takes a whiff. "Armocita, the scent of you is gratifying."

She smears her ass down his nose and rests it over his mouth. He massages and slaps her ass cheeks. "Umm, your ass is bubbly and round."

He rolls his tongue around his mouth, pinches her cheek, and slides the tip of his tongue into her ass.

She looks over her shoulder, smiles, and grinds her ass into his face. "Eat that ass. Suck the life force from me."

He spreads her ass cheeks and bobs his head up and down. Armocita mutters, "eat this cupcake. You love tasting my chocolate icing. Dig deeper until I cream on your tongue."

He pulls his face away and inserts a finger into her asshole and another in her pussy.

"Oh, shit," she moans as his fingers dig through her holes. She clinches her ass and pussy simultaneously, praying she can grip his fingers tighter.

He slides his fingers out and strips out his clothes.

Armocita sees Devastation staring at her, hoping she didn't bite off more than she could chew.

Devin clamps his hands over Devastation and strokes his hand up and down. "Are you sure you want this in your asshole?"

"Spit in my ass and fuck me," she commands.

Devin stoops downs, spits twice in her asshole, and substitutes Devastation in place of his fingers.

He eases the tip of his head inside. Armocita jerks and grunts.

"Are you ok?" he asks.

"Umm, mmm."

He slowly pokes her entrance and slides his inches a little at a time.

To Devin's surprise, Armocita's asshole loosens. He straddles his legs on either side of her waist and slowly slides his dick back and forth.

He leans over and kisses the side of her cheek. "Bitch, you are about to get all this dick. Do you understand me? You better brace yourself. Devastation is coming."

He pushes her chest and face into the sofa.

He speeds up his penetrations. She moans as he slaps her ass cheeks. "Shut up, bitch."

He grabs the side of her waist, yanking her back to meet his strokes. He jerks and strokes harder. She screams, "ahh, ahh, ahh."

She closes her eyes and grimaces but refuses to tell him to stop.

He pumps faster, gliding his ass in the air and slamming his dick inward.

He places his head between her shoulder blades and focuses on catching his nut.

He pounds more brutally and ignores Armocita's screams. "Shut up! You wanted this dick. Beg for me to cum. Tell me to cream pie this asshole."

"Do it, baby. Do it, please!" she begs.

He huffs, grunts, and fucks her more robustly than before. He bites down on his teeth, tightens his ass, his body shivers, and his dick strokes intensify.

He becomes quiet for a second.

"Ahh shit!" he shrieks.

Armocita feels Devin's nut sailing into her asshole. He thrusts and shakes until he empties everything inside of her.

He slides his dick out and rolls to the other side of the sofa. He is having a hard time trying to catch his breath.

"Whew, Devin! That shit was amazing. Excuse me while I shower. Your kids are jumping from my ass and parachuting down my legs."

She jumps from the sofa and disappears into her bedroom. "Make yourself at home," she yells.

Devin looks down at Devastation and slaps it. "She tried to give us a run for our money, but in the end, we are always victorious."

Chapter 21

Devin huffs and puffs before knocking on Ms. Shantae's door. He prays he's not here long because the proposal for his client is due tomorrow morning.

"It's open," Ms. Shantae yells from behind the cracked door.

He walks in and slides a chair next to her desk. "Ms. Shantae, unlike the other students, I can manage my addiction. If you would kindly sign my graduation certificate, I promise to stay out of trouble."

Ms. Shantae holds the palm of her hand in the air. "What's rule number one of Whore Rehab, Mr. Williams?"

"Leave your narcissistic ways at home," they recite together.

His lips quivered, and he was tempted to start a debate. Instead, he runs his fingers through his locs and leans back in his chair.

She stares into his eyes without flinching or saying a word. He knew she wasn't about to entertain his bullshit today.

She waves her index finger from side to side. "Devin, you can pour the sweetest perfume on a whore, and they will still smell like cum. A downfall is coming. And the pain will cripple your finances and your Zulu warrior physique."

His smile widens when he hears the compliment on his body.

"Mr. Williams, put away your self-centered ambitions for a minute. Are you ready for the truth?"

"It depends on the version you are about to release."

She balls her fist and slams it on top of the desk. "You are addicted to buying pussy because you fear your little heart will stop beating again.

"Stop being a fucking coward. Every woman is not your ex. You can accomplish a healthy relationship in the future if you give love another round, even if you don't want to find love. How about abstaining from sex?"

He jumps from his seat and shouts, "give up sex? Come on, Ms. Shantae, you are asking for things I can't live without. This time last year, I was buying pussy twice a day. Now, I'm down to three girls a week. I believe that's an improvement."

She shakes her head. "Do you hear the words coming out of your mouth?"

She types on her keyboard and returns to their conversation.

"May I ask what you are writing?"

"Progress notes for me to review. What difference does it make?"

She stands from her chair and walks around the room.

She pimp-walked through the room, waving her hand by her side and dragging her left leg. "Allow me to demonstrate your personality.

"I'm big, bad Devin Williams. I barely buy pussy. It's not an addiction. I'm not a whore, but if someone asked me to stop, I get offended and blame my ex-girlfriend."

"Real funny, Ms. Shantae."

She laughs while making her way back to her seat.

"Devin, why did you schedule this session today? You're not interested in graduating or changing your lifestyle."

His phone vibrates, and without looking, he accidentally clicks the answer button instead of denying the call.

He begins his conversation with Ms. Shantae without realizing there's someone on the other end of the cell phone.

"Ms. Shantae, there is something that is bothering me. I have a big decision to make, and time is running out."

"Okay, you have my undivided attention. Is this off the record, or does it matter?" she asks.

"It doesn't matter. My job has offered me an opportunity to work in Beijing. A part of me is ready, and the other half is scared.

"Before I became Vee's sponsor, I would have caught a flight as soon as my boss considered me. I'm not too sure I can leave her.

"We are in a beautiful place and leaving her right now might wreck her life. What if she flips out if I'm not around to sponsor her?"

"Devin, have you and Vee been intimate?"

He mumbles, "no," and quickly shouts, "hell no!"

She slides her glasses down the bridge of her nose. "Are you sure?"

"Ms. Shantae, I promise, we have never fucked. We had a few solo adventures, and I allowed her to spend the night while we watched Criminal Minds. Other than that, I have been a great sponsor.

"I can't pinpoint my emotions, but I miss her when she's not around."

"Do you have chemistry and emotions with the other ladies you see?"

"I ate some ass last week if that count. Have to believe in chemistry to open a woman's butt cheeks."

"Devin, if I were a regular therapist, I would put you out of my office. But since I understand your excitement about buying sex, I'll allow you to continue. Who is this woman?"

"Armocita. Oh my God, tasting her is like sipping wine from the Holy Grail. She is fantastic, beautiful, intelligent, and ambitious, but I couldn't see myself dating her."

"May I ask why?"

"Age doesn't matter to me, but she needs a man who can spark her dreams. A man willing to marry her heart, soul, and mind. I will never be able to offer any woman those things."

He gags louder to interrupt the thought of marriage. "I wish I could take a shit on every engagement ring known to man. Fuck a proposal. Walking down the aisle is bullshit."

"Devin, I want you to complete another homework assignment before you consider taking your new job."

"Sure, I'm down for another challenge. What is it this time?"

"I want you to meet with your ex and get closure."

He pulls his locs again, exhales out his mouth, and shakes his head in disgust. "Of all the challenges, you want me to return to that funky-ass bitch?"

Ms. Shantae laughs and puts her hand on Devin's knuckles. "Listen, self-healing comes when the soul's ties are broken."

"Okay, Ms. Shantae, I'll give it a shot."

"That's all I can ask of you. I promised the light at the end will be glorious."

"I trust your advice. You have been a tremendous help over the years."

She stands from her seat. "I can help more if you stop skipping our sessions."

He smiles and walks toward the door. "You are right. And if I decide to take the job, you better be available for a zoom call."

"What's my second rule?"

"Leave no whore behind," they recite.

He leaves the building and pulls out his phone to order an Uber.

He holds his breath and places his fist against his mouth. *Shit*, he thinks to himself.

He realizes he tapped the answer button on the phone earlier, and Vee has been listening to his whole conversation.

"Vee, why are you still on the phone with your nosy ass?"

"Well, I wanted to treat you to dinner. I kept saying hello, but you never responded. Then I overheard the conversation and felt compelled to listen."

"Whatever, Vee. Some things are personal. Your ass should have hung up."

"Since I've got you on the phone, come and get me."

"I'm sure you are around the corner somewhere."

"You know me so well," she reminds him and hangs up the phone.

FLENARDO

Chapter 22

Vee watches Joe as he marks his territory in five different spots. She yanks on the leash. "Hurry the hell up and pee, Joe!" she yells.

Joe ignores her command. She walks toward his direction to fuss at his hard-headed ass. After a few steps, her phone rings, and she taps her Beats Studio buds.

"Hello, who's this?"

"Is that any way to chat with an old friend?"

"Old dirty-ass friend," she implies while grinding her teeth. "We always agreed to share the woman, but you decided to sneak behind me and fuck Laura alone.

"The worst part was the night I ate her out while you fucked her. She came, and you came, but I went to sleep with a dry and angry pussy!

"If your lying ass didn't want to fuck, all you had to do was say so instead of blaming me for your dick not getting hard."

"Sorry, Vee, I will make it up to you. Let's work out together again, and we can talk about it."

"Work out with this!" she yells, tapping her buds to disconnect the call.

She pulls Joe into the house, gives him a treat, and prepares to begin her morning DIY project.

A customer from Facebook marketplace has commissioned her to build a bookshelf for her five-year-old daughter.

She ties and wraps her hair up with a durag. She changes into some old coveralls with paint stains from the last project.

She memorizes the instructions from the YouTube tutorials, grabs her jigsaw, and cuts the wood in a curvy shape.

She retrieves the nails and gorilla glue from the toolkit to stabilize the shelves. She unrolls the banding she purchased from Home Depot, places them over the edges of the frame, and sands down the rough patches.

After repeating the task for every shelf and nailing it together, she paints the bookshelf with a can of Berry Pink Rust-Oleum.

Once the bookshelf dries, she adds some stuffed animals and books from Walmart. She takes a photo and sends it to the customer.

DEVASTATION

Moments later, the customer responds with a thank you message followed by the payment plus tip.

Vee messages the customer her home address while walking into the bathroom. She undresses, turns on the shower, and plans the rest of the day inside her head.

I could stay home and write in my diary. I have missed a few entries, and my pages deserve to be as wet as my fat pussy. Umm, maybe I should run this showerhead between my thighs.

Stop it, Vee, get a hold of yourself. You promised to slow down and not fuck all the time.

Okay, I'll call Devin's fine ass and see what he's doing. I'm angry about his new opportunity in Beijing, but who am I to stop someone from living their dream? I pray I will be okay while he's out of the country.

Maybe I'll finish my shower and give one of these guys on my Tinder dating app an opportunity to meet me in person.

Yeah, that would be wonderful. I hope this guy dresses better than the last guy I dated.

She finds an opportunity to escape boredom and imagines meeting and dating a nice guy for a change.

She washes her hair, finishes showering, and grabs the hairdryer on her way out of the bathroom.

She flops on the bed, grabs her iPad, and searches Tinder for a potential match.

She deletes the profiles of all the men that sent her a dick pic without her permission.

After reading *The Three Worst Types of Unsolicited Dick Pic* by Katy Lana Hall, she has become more aware of her interaction with men.

She adds another website tab and refreshes her memory by rereading the article. There's the BASIC BITCH or FUCKBOY. Usually, it's your ex or someone you used to fuck.

The second one is the BLINDSIDE. You can discuss what's for dinner, and they will text a dick pic. So fucking gross.

The third and worst culprit is the old fashion LET DOWN, which consists of a disappointing dick pic.

"I'm a nympho and wouldn't suck or spin on that little shit."

She laughs harder while thinking about how many pictures she has stumbled upon using Tinder.

A request pops up as she deletes her final profile. It's from one of the most respectable guys she has met on the app.

DEVASTATION

She has never shared unsolicited pictures or spoken about sex with the six-foot-three, dark chocolate man named Julius.

She never accepted his date for fear of disaster striking before they could share dessert.

"What do I have to lose?" she questions herself.

She types her cell number and asks him to call her to discuss a meetup.

The phone rang, and she answered, "hello."

"Good afternoon, Vee. It's a pleasure to hear your voice."

She gasps for air from hearing his deep voice. Her pussy and heart jump instantaneously.

She clears her throat and bashfully responds, "likewise."

He says, "I know a beautiful place with great music and drinks. Have you ever heard of BB's Jazz, Blues, and Soup?"

"Fuck," she mumbles her breath.

That place is for Devin and me, she reminds herself.

She quickly suggests another location. "It's funny you asked because the girls and I went there the other night."

"I am late, but I'm sure we can find an alternative place to get to know each other. How about we meet at The Fountain on Locust?"

"Wow, cool name. I have never heard of it and have been in St. Louis for a while now."

"Yes, many people overlook the restaurant, but they have some of the best events in the city. This week, they have the Wall Ball."

"Sounds interesting, but I don't know what you are talking about."

"It's an event where artists will create art right before your eyes. You can observe and place a bid on the silent auction."

"Aww shit! Are there any gothic or skulls artists there?" she excitedly asks.

"I'm not sure, but I guarantee you will have fun. I'll bid on the first painting, and I know you will fall head over heels for it."

"Wow, you are sexy and a gentleman."

"Oh, you find me sexy? Why, thank you."

There goes that deep voice again, she thinks to herself.

She places her hand between her legs and clamps her thighs together. She feels the moisture sliding and quickly thinks of something else before masturbating.

"Okay, I can meet you there at seven-thirty," she yells.

He laughs and calmly states, "perfect."

"See you later tonight, Julius."

"Be safe, and I'll be anticipating your arrival."

They disconnect the call, and she stretches across the bed. She visualizes her date with Julius and is pleased he's respectable and has manners.

She grabs her phone, calls Devin's number, and waits on him to answer.

"What's good?"

"This pussy, if you weren't so afraid of it," she answers.

She didn't wait for a comeback and explained her reasons for calling. "Devin, I'm going out on a date, and this guy is a gentleman."

"Please don't change your Facebook relationship status after a week of knowing him."

"Asshole! For your information, I've been chatting with him for a few months before I even agreed to go on this date."

"Do you need me to hack into his account and see if he has any skeletons?" he asks.

"No, I don't. I need to find someone to date before you take the job overseas and leave me for some Chinese pussy.

"If I'm committed to one man, maybe, just maybe, I can stop fucking random people and deadbeat exes."

"You sound ridiculous, Vee."

"And you sound jealous. Always pretending like you are perfect."

"I'm far from perfect. I need you to slow down and perform background checks on people you meet on these social apps."

"Yeah, yeah, yeah. I've heard that before. You need to be ready to watch Criminal Minds next week. I got this, boo boo."

"Alright, Vee. Just be careful and don't drink too much. You know how you are."

"Aww, you do care. Okay, I have to get ready. Talk to you later."

DEVASTATION

Chapter 23

'Turn right' was her GPS's command as Vee approached Locust Street. She turns, coasts the car, and looks for a parking place.

'You have arrived,' the GPS speaks.

She notices a guy leaning against the parking meter holding a skull-potted plant head with roses inside.

"She rolls down her window. Are you saving this spot for anyone?"

"Vee, it's me. Julius."

"I'm sorry, skulls always kidnap my attention. Let me back up, and I'll park, then we can go inside."

Nice gesture. One Point for Mr. Julius, she thinks to herself.

She flips down the visor, checks her makeup, grabs her purse, and right before she reaches for the door handle, Julius opens the door. "A woman will never have to open her car door when she's around me. I would have offered to park your car, but you whipped into the parking space too quickly."

"It's a habit, plus my car is a lesbian named Abby. She doesn't like men sitting their asses on her face."

He laughs while clutching her hand and lifting her from the seat. "You can leave the roses in the car until we return."

They interlock their fingers and walk towards the restaurant, hand in hand.

She admires Julius' linen blend two-button jacket and pantsuit. He wore a sky-blue collar shirt and a pair of brown leather Oxford shoes.

Point number two, she thinks and smiles at the same time.

He opens the door, places his hand on the lower part of her back, and escorts her inside.

They walk through the restaurant, and Vee notices everyone's eyes are upon them. She feels free and beautiful, like a princess from a Disney movie.

Julius leans closer to her ear. "Are you ready for tonight?"

"I hope so."

"Great. I contacted an artist to create something magical for you."

He leads her down the hallway, and she overhears music from a lighted room about fifty feet away.

DEVASTATION

"This place is different," she replies.

"Yes, it is, but you haven't seen anything yet. Close your eyes, and you can't open until I allow you to."

She squeezes her eyes and his hand tight, hoping she doesn't trip as she walks.

"Open," he whispers.

She opens her eyes and sees a crowded room yelling, "surprise!"

She smiles at Julius and kisses his cheek. In her soft voice, she thanked him for the beautiful gesture.

There was a giant painting of two skeletons dancing inside a spiral whirlwind. The vibrant and colorful image captures her mind.

"Go ahead and touch it. It's yours. I had a special friend paint it for you since you love skulls and gothic art."

She walks up to the artwork and runs her fingers over the painting like she would the tip of her clit. She can't wait to take it home, hang it on the wall, and masturbate while staring at it.

She buries the vision in the rear of her mind and returns her attention to Julius. "I'm honored, but you didn't have to do all these beautiful things."

"It was my pleasure to make you smile. You need daily happiness, and I'm the man to fulfill it."

His deep voice and cologne are perfect for him to crawl in this pussy tonight, she thinks to herself.

She doesn't comprehend anything he is saying but watches his lips move, which makes her wetter.

She walks up to him, stands on her tiptoes, and kisses him in the crowded room.

He pulls away and backs up a few steps. "I wasn't expecting a tongue wrestling match."

"Was it too much?" she asks.

"No, it was perfect, but save some for later. People are staring."

"Are you afraid of a little public affection?"

"No, not at all. But I do like to keep my business discreet with the women I date. Now let's go to the table, sip a little wine, and listen to some music."

He introduces her to a few friends as they part through the crowd to sit at their table.

Vee notices the winks and fist pounds from some of Julius' male friends. A few women showcase their evil smirks combined with 'you don't belong here' stares.

She pulls Julius closer as they walk, alerting everyone he's taking for the evening.

They sit, and Vee observes the artists as they paint with various colors and slow strokes on the canvas.

She wonders if their passion for painting is equivalent to lovemaking.

She has been fucked numerous times but never touched sensually. Men love her pussy but never love the woman that comes with the pussy.

She tears up, grabs a napkin, and pats her eyes before her makeup is ruined.

"Are you ok?" Julius asks.

Fuck, he noticed, she thought.

"I'm fine, just something in my eye."

He leans closer, opens her left eyelid, and blows in her eyes like she's a little girl.

"Whatever was in there, it's all gone now," he said.

She giggles and taps his leg. "Thanks for being such a gentleman. I'm going to the restroom to check on my makeup. I'll return shortly."

"You look adorable to me. Please hurry back. I'll keep your seat warm for you."

She slides out of the booth. "Thanks again."

She stands and turns her head over her shoulder. "My stomach has been growling since I stepped out of the car. Can you order the royal grille cheese with turkey and a glass of honey whiskey?"

"Sure, will there be anything else?"

"Yes, you. Especially if you keep acting like my future husband."

She walks away and asks one of the servers where the restroom is. She follows the directions and pushes the door open.

A few women are chatting and checking their makeup. She finds a space between them and applies some lipstick.

The stall door behind her opens, and a woman wearing a beanie cap, flannel shirt, and ripped jeans steps out.

She approaches the sink, and the other ladies leave the restroom. Vee notices and thinks it's awkward but is not shaken by the woman.

She twists the skulls on her necklace and checks the time on her watch. *Guess I'll head back to the table with Julius,* she thinks.

She turns towards the door, and the baggy woman cuts her off.

"Why are you with him?" the baggy woman asks.

"Who the hell are you talking about?"

"Stop playing games. That sick pig, Julius."

"Look, I don't know you, and Julius is wonderful. Better than most men I have met in the past few years."

"Whatever. My name is Jessica, and I'm one of the featured artists. I'm going to assume you are new to this circle, and I can't share everything with you due to my confidentiality agreement."

"Are you one of his exes?" Vee asks.

"I wish I could say what I am. Listen, go home, and stay away from Julius."

"As I said before, I don't know you, so I'm returning to my table."

She bumps her shoulder against Jessica's and walks out the restroom door.

She goes to the table, slides back into her seat, sips her whiskey, and ignores the conversation with Jessica.

This bitch is jealous because she's not getting any attention, she thinks.

She snuggles closer to Julius as the venue dims the lights for the glow-in-the-dark painting exhibition.

He kisses her cheek and massages her shoulders. "Thanks for coming out with me. Tonight will be a night you will forever remember."

FLENARDO

Chapter 24

Vee's emotions were at an implausible high during the Wall Ball. Julius introduced her to some of the finest artists in St. Louis.

She left an everlasting impression on them when she opened her phone and gave them a show and tell of her gothic jewelry.

One of the artists gave Vee their contact information and asked if she was interested in displaying her jewelry at their gallery.

She would have conversed with them all night if Julius hadn't snuck up behind her and squeezed her waist.

"Do you mind if I steal her away?" he asks.

The group thanked her for coming to the ball and continued chatting.

"Wow! I can't believe you invited me to this enchanted place. I can't wait to tell my best friend," she brags.

"Well, the night is just beginning. There's an afterparty at The Angad Arts Hotel, and you will love the ambiance. I only have one question for you."

She winks her eye. "Sure, I can answer anything that comes from your mouth."

"Red, Green, Blue, or Yellow?" he asks.

"Umm, I love all those colors. But after the fun I had tonight, I'll be spontaneous and say red."

"Perfect choice because I have a one bedroom, 1.5 bath, grand suite with a separate living and dining room to explore until the sun rises."

"And the room is red?" she asks.

"Aww, that's the surprise. The hotel manager told me the red color stands for empowerment, finding your purpose, and moving forward with creative decisions," he explains.

She swings his arm over her shoulders and kisses his face while talking in between words. "I can't wait," she kisses him. "To see this hotel room," another kiss. "Because I feel empowered already," and another kiss.

"Terrific! That's the excitement I want to hear from you," he said.

"Before the show, one of my friends asked to use my car. Is it okay if I ride with you to the hotel?"

Vee smiles and responds, "absolutely!"

They hold hands and chat about the artists while walking to her car.

Julius thanks her for letting him meet the most beautiful woman he has ever seen.

She absorbs his flattering compliments. Tonight, she feels extraordinary but wonders if this moment is too good to be true.

"Julius, you are the first man that has made me feel worthy in a long time. If you are playing games, just fuck me and send me home. I'm used to guys treating me that way."

He grabs her hand. "Vee, stop selling yourself short. I plan on treating you with the utmost respect. I'm looking for a potential wife because girlfriends are for little boys who like playing with a girl's emotions."

She smiles, and deep down, her soul screams, *yes!*

Julius guides Vee to her driver's seat. "Buckle up, baby. You're about to go for the ride of your life."

He closes the door, and she watches him through the rearview mirror. *That man is fine as a muthafucka*, she thinks.

He opens the passenger door, slides in the SUV, and leans over to taste her lips.

After breaking away from a romantic kiss, Vee starts the car and drives toward the hotel.

Julius turns on the radio and sings some verses from *Tank's No Limit* song.

Vee hums along, attempting to distract him long enough so he wouldn't notice her legs shaking.

They listen to a few more songs until they arrive in the hotel parking lot.

The night air blows on her neck. She shivers, and Julius, once again, comes to her rescue. He pulls his jacket from under his arm and wraps it around Vee as they walk to the hotel entrance.

Once inside, she notices the abstract art on the walls and people's fashionable clothes. Everyone appears to be on some euphoric journey with no stress from the outside world.

Julius and Vee stop at the elevator door, and he presses the up button. The doors open, and they are welcomed inside with smooth jazz music.

Julius presses the second-floor button. "Vee, I'm not sure if you know this, but the number 2 is known to numerologists as a supreme feminine force representing grace and power."

She blushes more than before. "No, I didn't know that, but thanks for providing insight."

They hum and dance until the elevator reaches the second floor.

He takes her hand and leads her to his suite. Once inside, he removes the jacket from Vee's shoulders. "Would you like something to drink? We have about thirty minutes before the afterparty begins."

"Sure. What do you have?"

"I know you are a whiskey woman, but tonight, let me introduce you to my favorite drink."

He walks to the refrigerator, opens the door, and reaches inside. "Devil Springs Vodka," he announces as he pulls the bottle from the fridge.

He grabs two glasses from the cabinet and looks over at Vee. "You are going to love this drink. One shot, and it's a one-way ticket to hell."

"Well, tell Satan I'm on my way with some gasoline drawers on," she jokes.

He laughs at her sense of humor and mixes the drink. Once satisfied, he dims the lights in the suite and hands her the glass.

"To a beautiful night for two incredible people," he toasts. They cling the glasses and sip the drinks while discussing their fun at the art party.

Ten minutes later, they giggle, drink more, and chat like lovebirds. Julius picks up the glasses from the nightstand and places them on the counter.

He grabs her hand. "Are you ready to go to the party, Vee?"

She sways from side to side and places her palm on her head. "Julius, what's…in…the drink?" she mumbles.

He stoops down in front of her face. "Vee, are you ok? You look dizzy, and you're slurring your words."

He pushes her forehead back, and she falls on the bed. "Maybe you should lie down," he suggests.

Her head is spinning, and the room is dark except for the clock on the nightstand, illuminating the time.

"Vee, Vee, Vee. I'm going to take care of you tonight. You are fading into another world.

"I have been dropping hints all night. I told you this would be a night to remember. I mention how one shot will take you to hell. In your case, it took about three, but who's counting?

"Don't fight back. I don't want to hurt you, but I will if I have to," he threatens.

He kisses her earlobe. "Bitch, do you understand me?"

Her brain tells her to fight, but her motor skills are dead. She attempts to shake her head and move her legs.

Nothing. She is captive to the man she thought was a gentleman.

"We all have an obsession, an addiction, and some will say we are sick in the head. You love to fuck. Well, I love raping slutty ass bitches.

"As I said before, I'm a gentleman. I won't tear your clothes. Hell, I won't even mess up your makeup."

He laughs before slipping off her shoes and dropping them to the floor. He lifted her torso, unbuttoned her dress from the back, and slid it over her head.

He removes his arm from behind her back, and her body flops onto the bed. He licks his lips, admiring her floral Victoria's Secret bra and panty set.

He traces his finger over her thigh, sticks it under her panties, and pushes it hard inside her pussy. He snatches it out and inhales the aroma. "At least your slutty ass smells good.

"Welcome to the red room. You thought you were about to be empowered? I'm going to teach you the meaning of being powerless. Tonight, I'm going to own your ass."

He stands up and strips out of his clothes.

Get up, Vee! You have to try to fight. Julius, get the hell off me! she yells in her mind.

Julius turns around and waves his dick in front of her face. He sticks three fingers in her mouth and pries her mouth open.

He runs the tip of his head over her bottom lip. "Yeah bitch, I'm going to fuck your mouth. Gotta teach whores like you a lesson."

He tugs on the shaft of his dick while smearing his dick head over her mouth. He forces her mouth wider, turns her head to the side, and fucks her throat.

He starts slow but increases his tempo as he slides his dick over her tongue and deeper down her throat for the next five minutes.

Once pleased with his deed, he stops and slides his dick out. "Wasn't that fun? You're having a great time, aren't you? Fucking you is the afterparty," he admits.

He laughs while sliding her panties over her knees and feet and tosses them over his right shoulder. He unbuttons her bra and places it over her face.

He bites her left nipple and squeezes her right nipple ring. "You love a man to play with your titties. You have big titties too."

He bites her nipples, clamping his teeth tighter, and grinds them from side to side.

He slaps her face. "Hey, zombie hoe. Do you want some dick?"

He laughs at his joke and whispers in her ear. "The drug you were sipping on is illegal in America. It can be fatal if you consume too much, but fortunately, I am a great mixer."

He turns her over onto her stomach, spreads open her legs, and kisses the middle of her back. "I'm going to fuck you in the ass and pussy until I cum in one of your holes. Are you okay with my decision?"

He mashes the palm of his hand on the back of her head and pushes her head up and down. "Yeah, I knew you would agree.

"Vee, I wasn't always a monster. Growing up, I didn't have much money, and women always rejected the broke, nice guy.

"Not anymore. I'm leveling the playing field."

He grinds his dick over the opening of her ass cheeks and runs it down to the back of her knees. "Do you feel how hard you are making me, Vee?"

He pokes the head of his dick at her clit. "Alright slut, are you ready to be fucked?" he asks.

He slaps her ass cheeks. "I can't wait to be inside of you. You're not worthy of being in a relationship. No respectable woman should be on Tinder. I have to punish thirsty bitches like you."

He slides his dick backward and creeps forward towards her pussy lips.

He takes a deep breath and forcefully penetrates her pussy. "Ahh, your shit is wet and warm. I can't wait to see what that asshole feels like."

He arches his back and glides his dick in and out of her pussy. "Ooh, Vee, I might cum in this hole first."

He yanks her hair, and her head lifts from the bed. "I want that ass now," he demands.

He slides his dick out of her pussy and sticks his fingers in her ass to loosen it up.

"It's tight, baby. Your asshole might be the only spot on your body you don't allow men to fuck often. We are going to change that."

His fingers dig deeper and deeper. He retrieves them and smells them. "Damn, tonight's my lucky night. Even your asshole smells good."

He licks his fingers. "No shit. Just wetness. Yeah, I'm going to rape all your holes tonight."

He probes her asshole with his tip, and pierces deep inside her. He grips the comforter with his nails for support.

"Oh shit, I'm unsure which hole I want to fill now."

He wraps a fist full of hair and heaves her head back. "Give me this ass. Please, give it to me."

He fucks her repeatedly for fifteen minutes before switching to her pussy.

He rotates between her pussy and asshole for thirty more minutes before indecisively nutting on her lower back.

He rolls over to the empty side of the bed and pats her ass cheek with his hand. "Relax, Vee. I'll fuck your zombie-looking ass again once I catch my second wind."

He stares at the ceiling and erupts with laughter. Before spreading her legs and eating her pussy from the back.

He smiles and whispers, "I'm one sick fuck."

FLENARDO

DEVASTATION

Chapter 25

Vee's nose twitches from the stench of alcohol seeping from Julius' pores. Her eyelids gradually open from a world of darkness, and she sees the sun beaming through the blind slats.

She wiggles her toes and fingers. "Okay, Vee, you have movement. Let's try to stand and get the fuck out of here," she whispers.

She turns her head to the clock. It's 6 am. Tears run from her eyes as she feels the cool air on her naked body. She looks around and sees her clothes on the floor.

She dangles her left leg off the bed. She turns her head to ensure Julius doesn't feel her scooting off the mattress.

She pauses for a second, takes a deep breath, and glides her other leg over. Once her feet hit the ground, she tiptoes over to her dress and picks it up, then quickly grabs her phone and keys.

She creeps to the door, unbolts the lock, and quietly slides out. Once outside, she dashes down the hall until she reaches the elevator.

She presses the down-button multiple times before the door opens. She slides into the corner, slips her dress on, and prays Julius is not standing in front of the elevator when she arrives on the first floor.

The elevator pings, and it seems like the door takes forever to open. Her heart beats faster, and her hands tremble.

She feels a sigh of relief escape her as no one is on the other side of the door. She races out of the hotel and through the parking lot, tapping her key fob until she hears her car alarm.

She locates her car and hits the button for the remote start. She jumps in the car, shifts the transmission to drive, and speeds out of the parking lot.

She activates the Siri control button from her steering wheel. "Call Kaylene!" she yells.

The phone rings as she speeds through a red light and travels to Kaylene's home.

"Hello," Kaylene answers.

"Throw on some clothes, bring me a pair of sandals, and meet me outside. I'm on my way to pick you up."

"What the fuck?" Kaylene responds.

"I can't explain right now. I'll be there real soon."

She disconnects the call and speeds through another traffic light. "Fuck! I hope the police are eating doughnuts and not waiting to give me a damn ticket."

She drives through Kaylene's residential neighborhood, bouncing over speed bumps and honking her horn at slower drivers.

She pulls up to the curb, and Kaylene jumps in the car. Before Kaylene could ask what was wrong, Vee yelled, "that bastard raped me!"

"Who?"

"Julius' nasty ass. I'm going to kill that muthafucker when I see him again."

Kaylene leans over and hugs Vee. "I know you are furious, but you can't throw your life away over this.

"If you had killed him before leaving the hotel, you could have claimed self-defense. I love you too much to visit you behind bars.

"Let's go to the police station and see what they can do," Kaylene suggests.

"Matter of fact, swap seats with me. I don't think you need to drive while you are in shock."

Kaylene runs around the car and waits on Vee to get in on the other side.

"Are you ready?" Kaylene asks.

"Yeah. Just take me to the police station, but I still want to shoot his ass."

Kaylene does her best to distract Vee as they ride. She didn't want her to think about the tragic experience.

During the conversation, Vee drifts off to sleep and wakes up when the car halts.

"We are at the Metropolitan Police Department. Let's go inside and talk to someone," Kaylene said.

They walk inside and approach the front desk. "Good morning, Officer. My friend Veronica would like to report a sexual assault."

The officer looks over at Vee. "Please sit, and I'll have the detective come right out. We will do everything we can to assist you."

Vee and Kaylene sit on the bench, and miraculously, a female detective comes out the door within five minutes.

"Hi, my name is Detective Anderson. Before escorting you to my office, can I offer you anything?"

Veronica shakes her head from side to side while Kaylene holds her hands.

"Okay, just checking. Well, let's go ahead and file an initial report," Detective Anderson said.

Vee let go of Kaylene's hand. "I'll be back. I'd rather not tell you all the details yet."

Kaylene hugs her and whispers, "I understand," in her ear.

Vee follows the detective through the door and down the hall until they stop in front of her office.

"Please come in and have a seat," Detective Anderson said.

"You caught me at the right time because my shift is about to end, but I have time to help you. I'm about to ask you some sensitive questions. Try to answer them as truthfully as you can."

Vee nods her head.

Detective Anderson grabs a pen and begins taking notes.

"Okay, Veronica. Can you tell me the person, the date, and the location of the assault?"

Vee explains how they met, how he drugged her, and how she didn't consent to have sex with him.

Detective Anderson writes Vee's details in her notepad and places her pen on her desk. "Ms. Veronica, you mentioned you met Julius on Tinder. Do you know his last name?"

Vee pauses for a second and tries to remember. She looks around the room and responds, "no, I don't."

"Ms. Veronica, I hate to ask this, but it's imperative. How often do you use dating apps for sexual hookups?"

Vee bites her lip and gives Detective Anderson a grimacing expression. "Why is that important?"

"If you decide to press charges and this goes to court, the prosecutor might subpoena you to turn over your laptop and other electronic devices. I understand you are the victim, but I need to know everything to protect you."

Vee stands from her seat. "So, I get raped, and you want to know how many guys I have fucked using dating apps? This is bullshit! I'm the one who was drugged and fucked all night. Barely able to move while this evil devil tormented my body."

"Veronica, please take a seat. I understand the frustration."

"No, you don't. I'm getting the fuck out of here. I'm not about to allow the world into my business."

Vee walks out of the office, down the hall, and rushes into Kaylene's arms. "This was a mistake. I should have never come here," she confides.

Kaylene brushes Vee's hair with her hand. "It's okay. I'll stay with you. It's not a good idea for you to be alone."

Vee cries on Kaylene's shoulder as they depart the precinct.

DEVASTATION

Kaylene puts Vee in the car, hugs her, and gets in the driver's seat.

Kaylene looks over at Vee. "Stay strong. You are going to heal from this. I'm not leaving you. Is there anyone you would like me to call?"

"I'm not in the mood to speak with anyone right now. Just take me home, and I'll take some pills to go to sleep."

Maybe I'll take the whole bottle and won't have to see tomorrow, she ponders.

FLENARDO

DEVASTATION

Chapter 26

Devin has called and texted Vee's cell phone for two weeks. Now her voicemail is full, and he cannot leave any more messages.

"Damn, where the hell are you, Vee?" She missed Criminal Minds date night last week and is a no-show for tonight.

He dials Ms. Shantae's phone and waits for her to answer.

"Good evening, Devin. How are you doing?"

"I'm concerned about Vee. Have you heard from her?"

"No, I haven't heard from her. I'll make some phone calls and see what I can find out. I'm sure she's okay."

"Thanks. Because this is not her norm," Devin responds.

Devin disconnects the call and clears his mind for a moment. "Yeah, I'm sure she's okay. Maybe she needed her space. I'll give her time to adjust."

He grabs his laptop and decides to hack into the OnlyFans paywall.

After ten minutes of scrolling and DM'ing some models, he quickly becomes bored with their conversations and logs off.

His stomach growls, reminding him that he only had a protein shake all day. He runs his hand over his stomach. "We need some meat."

He locks up his penthouse and goes downtown. While walking, he passes several restaurants and a Turkish restaurant called Aya Sofia.

The outside hostess smiles and waves to him. "Tonight, the special is grilled swordfish steak with sautéed spinach. And if that's not tempting enough, Nuray, our featured belly dancer, will have you drooling food out the side of your mouth."

"Now, you have my attention. Seating for one, please," he requests.

He follows the hostess inside, and she sits him at a two-seater table closer to the center of the floor.

Three minutes later, a beautiful brunette woman dressed in a Princess Jasmine outfit approaches his table. "Welcome to Aya Sofia. Did you have a chance to review the drink menu?"

"No, you zoomed in on your magic carpet before I could scan the menu," he smiles and replies. "Please bring me your finest bottle of Pinot Grigio."

"Gladly, I'll be back shortly." She turns around and disappears behind the bar.

He grabs his phone and text, *where are you?* to Vee. He holds his phone, anticipating the three dots to start blinking.

"Excuse me. Do you have room for one more?"

He looks up, and his pulse starts racing as he stares at the woman who should have been his wife.

A piece of him wants to act like an ass in this restaurant, but he can't risk going to jail or losing money over an old flame.

He stands from his seat and pulls out the empty chair. "You always had a way of being selfish. I'm sure you don't need my permission to join me.

"Simone, what are you doing here?"

"I'm visiting my mother," she replies and sits in the empty seat in front of him. "I saw you when you first walked in, and I had to come over here and talk to you."

She grabs his hands and says, "Devin."

He slides his hands away from hers. "Simone, before you say anything. You should listen."

They lock eyes with each other, and even with all the pain she has caused him, he's still attracted to her espresso-brown skin. Her teeth are white and perfect, her locs have grown three inches further down her back, and she still has a slim waistline and a fat ass.

"Sir, here's your bottle of Pinot," the server announces and interrupts Devin's infatuation.

Perfect timing because Simone's energy makes me vulnerable, he thinks to himself.

"Thank you. Can you bring another glass for my friend who won't be here long?

"You are forever gorgeous, and I can tell you are taking care of your outer appearance. How's that dark heart of yours doing?"

She stands from her chair. "Devin, I can tell this was a mistake."

He reaches over and squeezes her wrist. "Sit your ass down," he mumbles under his breath so no one in the restaurant will notice.

He snatches his hand from her wrist as the server returns with another glass and walks away.

"It's funny you are here because my therapist asked me to find closure. I don't want your apology, nor an explanation.

"Because of you, I don't trust women."

He chuckles and pours a glass of wine for her and himself—"cheers to the closure you never gave me."

He drinks the entire glass and sits it on the table. "As I said, I don't trust women because of you. I'm out here spending 15% of my salary on pussy.

"I'm afraid to open my heart because all I see is you on your knees, sucking that nigga's dick."

"Devin, that's enough. You aren't about to talk to me like that. You have every right to be angry at me. I'm mad at myself for cheating on you."

"What did he have over me?" Devin asks.

"Nothing."

"Well, why did you do it then?"

"Devin, I was young, stupid, and materialistic. Too impatient to understand your dreams and the life you were building for us. During that time, I was in love with the idea that fast money was better than a healthy relationship."

"Simone, I wish you had waited for me."

"Me too. Because I will never find another Devin Williams."

"Simone, my therapist said healing comes after the pain. I haven't seen you in years, and I despise the word marriage."

He exhales and runs his fingers through his locs. "I can't hold on to this negative energy any longer. I have to stop blaming you. I forgive you, Simone," he empathizes.

"Thank you, Devin. I've waited for what seems like an eternity to hear those words."

"Are you seeing anyone?" Devin asks.

"No. I have been single for a while now. After our breakup, I pursued my dreams and traveled the world as a flight attendant. I'm also one semester away from getting my degree in pre-med."

Devin claps his hands. "Impressive. I'm sure you will have your pediatric practice in the near future.

"Flight attendant, huh? I'm sure seeing you walking down the aisle in your uniform is causing the cabinet pressure to rise," he jokes.

The server returns with Devin's entrée, and Simone attempts to leave to rejoin her friends.

"I will allow you to eat peacefully, but my flight doesn't leave until six o'clock tomorrow evening."

She grabs his phone, types in her contact, and slides the phone to him. "Tell Devastation I said hello, and Mommy would love one last ride for old-time sake."

Chapter 27

"Devin called me today, and I don't feel comfortable lying to him. He already has trust issues with women, and I'm not trying to become his enemy."

"If you'd like, I can go with you tonight, and we can talk about everything that is happening with you."

Vee rocks back and forth on the couch without saying a word.

"Veronica Marie Hemsley, we will not wallow in this pain. We will fight your attacker and your fears."

Ms. Shantae walks over to the couch and hugs Vee. "Your life is not over."

She sniffs her nose and wipes away the tear that is running down her cheek. "Okay, I'll stop running and speak to him. Of all the men I have known, Devin has never judged me."

Ms. Shanta pats Vee's back. "Are you sure you don't want me to come?"

"No, you have done enough. I appreciate you and Kaylene for helping me get through this."

"This is how a family should love and support each other. In the morning, I'm going to call my friend at PAVSA. She's an attorney, and I'll see what she can do to help us with the legal system."

Ms. Shantae squeezes Vee tighter. "I love you, girl."

"Love you too," Vee replies.

Ms. Shantae stands to her feet and swings her purse over her shoulder. "If you need me, call."

"Sure," Vee responds.

Vee walks Ms. Shantae to the door and stands in the doorway until Ms. Shantae cranks up her car and leaves.

Vee closes the door and walks to the bathroom. She stares at the image in the mirror. "Damn, I look like shit."

She undresses, turns on the shower, and thinks of a way to explain her disappearance to Devin.

It's still Thursday. Maybe we could talk after the show if I show up for an episode of Criminal Minds, she thinks.

The steam from the shower fogs the mirror. She takes her index finger and spells 'SURVIVOR' before the mist evaporates.

She turns the water temperature down, steps in, and whispers, "thank you, God."

The night she left the police station, Kaylene spent the night sleeping in Vee's bed to keep an eye on her. Vee woke up to take an early morning piss. She opened her medicine cabinet and couldn't find her Valium.

She wanted to overdose the pain away. She knew Kaylene probably hid them, so she went and grabbed her .9mm and sat at the kitchen table.

Kaylene stumbled out of the room and caught Vee attempting suicide. She ran over and snatched the gun away. "You're not leaving me, Vee! What the fuck were you thinking?"

Vee snaps out of her flashback after feeling the cold water on her skin. "Shit, how long have I been standing in this shower? I have to call maintenance again. Damn water never stays hot."

She takes a cold shower and throws on some tights, a sweatshirt, and running shoes. She packs an overnight bag and she'll just take a hot bath at Devin's house.

She calls his phone, but there's no response. "I'm sure Mr. Gray will allow me to go in like always."

She pats Joe on the head. "Be a good boy, and I'll see you in the morning."

She drives over to Devin's penthouse and parks along the street. She grabs her overnight bag, locks her door, and enters the building.

"Good evening, Mr. Gray. Can you buzz me upstairs to see Mr. Williams?"

"Sure thing. We have been waiting on you to show up again. He left a clear message to let you up so he could cuss you out for not answering your phone."

He smiles and asks, "have you run into any bicycles lately?"

"Everyone is a comedian these days. Real funny, Mr. Gray. Real funny.

"That bicycle debacle was one of the best days of my life. Enjoy your evening, and I'll come down here to chat with you tomorrow."

"I am looking forward to it. Have a lovely night, Ms. Hemsley."

She rides the elevator upstairs and knocks on Devin's door. He answers and invites her into the penthouse.

"I'm glad you came tonight, of all night."

"Why is that?"

"I was seriously thinking about fucking my ex," he admits.

"The one that cheated on you and left you holding the engagement ring? I'm sure that would have cost you a fortune."

"Actually, I was going to fuck her without spending a dime."

She thinks, *Good thing I came tonight. I might have lost my chance forever with him if they had rekindled their romance.*

"Enough of my adventures. Where the hell have you been for the past two weeks? I thought you were dead, kidnapped, or in a coma. You can't have my mind bothered like that again. Do you understand me?" he asks.

"Yes, but can a woman have a seat first? You are chastising me and haven't even invited me inside yet."

"My bad, Vee. I had to get that out of my system."

She takes her bags to the guest room and reappears with a Michael Myer T-shirt and Halloween color socks.

"Would you like something to drink?" Devin asks.

"No, I'll fix my drink," she said.

"Sit down. You are a guest in my home. I got this."

She raises her foot from the ground and pulls her knees to her chest while sitting on the sofa.

Devin notices and walks over to sit beside her. "Vee, are you ok?"

She leans her head on his chest. "No, I'm not. I don't think I will ever be."

"What are you talking about?"

"Devin, remember the night I told you I was going out with the guy I thought was a gentleman?"

"Yeah, the one I wanted to do a background check on, but you were bragging about how you can take care of yourself."

"Yeah, that guy. I won't explain the details, but I was drugged and raped."

He pushes her away. "Whoa! I wasn't expecting you to tell me something like that. Did you go to the police or the hospital for a rape kit?"

"I went to the police, but they mentioned if I pressed charges, the court and lawyers would bring up my sexual past and the numerous guys I have fucked."

"Let it be exposed, then. That guy needs to pay for what he has done to you."

"Can we skip this conversation and watch Criminal Minds?" she asks.

"I'm not about to watch a TV show while your assailant is out there walking free."

"Devin, I would like to put it behind me. I'll be okay, eventually."

"Well, I won't."

He grabs her hand and takes her to his office. "Log in to your Tinder account and give me this guy's name."

"Devin, I assure you I'll be fine, eventually."

"Vee, stop talking foolishly and give me his name."

She has never seen Devin this angry. His hand is shaking, and the veins in his forearms are popping up thick.

She retrieves his name and passes it to Devin.

"Vee, I'm sorry for what happened to you. I promise Julius Winston will not get away with this. Go ahead and get some rest. I have to send his info to a friend who owes me a favor."

FLENARDO

DEVASTATION

Chapter 28

Julius sips his drinks while leaning against the tv stand. The bulge in his pants hardens as he lusts over the blonde woman he drugged for his weekend obsession.

He takes another sip, places the glass down, and licks his lips. "Yeah, this dumb bitch was throwing drinks down her throat like her stomach was on fire.

"What woman wears six-inch heels, a short mini skirt, and a long sleeve halter top that stops three inches above her navel?"

He walks over, slides his fingers between the strands of her hair, and sniffs the warm hints of cardamon, pineapple, and citrus lavender shampoo.

"I'm going to take my time with you," he whispers in her ear.

He turns around, grabs his phone, and searches the playlist for a song to start the party.

He plays *Blurred Lines by Robin Thicke* and begins singing the chorus while removing his clothes.

'Ok, now he was close
Tried to domesticate you

FLENARDO

But you're an animal
Baby, it's in your nature
Just let me liberate you
You don't need no papers
That man is not your maker
And that's why I'm gon' take a good girl
I know you want it
I know you want it'

He sings and strokes his dick as he walks over toward her. He slaps his dick across her face.

'I know you want it
'Cuz you're a good girl
Everybody getup'

"Oh, my bad. You can't get it up because you are my zombie whore," he jokes and laughs to himself.

He lifts her halter top above her breasts and circles her areole with two fingers. He stops and sticks his fingers in his mouth. "Umm. Umm. Finger licking good.

"Let's see what's else you have in the kitchen. I hope you don't mind if I peep in your cupboard."

He trails his hand down her chest and blows his breath over her navel.

He reaches under her skirt and pinches her thighs as he travels toward her juice bowl.

DEVASTATION

He stretches farther, and his fingers graze a soft, thick, meaty flesh. He snatches his hand from under her skirt. "What the fuck? This bitch got a dick!" he yells.

The blonde woman's eyes pop open, and Julius springs away from her and lands on the floor. He scooted backward until he was against the wall.

The balcony door slides open, and a female walks in, laughing and pointing a gun at Julius.

"Don't stop now. Go ahead and play with that dick. Get it real hard so we can put it in your mouth," she proclaims.

The woman from the balcony shakes her head in disgust at Julius. "Your dumb ass was anxious to drug and rape a woman tonight. You didn't even check your room to see if you were alone. Amateur muthafucka."

The woman from the balcony looks at the blonde on the bed. "Trinity, it looks like his dick has shriveled up. Show him what a real dick looks like."

Trinity lifts her skirt, licks the palm of her hands, and plays with her dick. "Asperilla, my cock will be hard in less than ten seconds."

"Listen, ladies. I'm sure we can work this out. I'm not into this gay shit," he admits.

"Why not? You love fucking bitches in the ass. Tonight, you will see what it feels like," Asperilla promises.

Outside the bedroom, they hear the door open and close in the suite.

"Looks like this party is about to get more interesting!" Asperilla proclaims.

Malakai walks in. "What did I miss?"

"How the hell y'all get in my room?" Julius questions.

"With your key card access. It's connected to our phone. Hotels should stop using all these apps you can hack into," Malakai confesses.

Malakai tosses Trinity some rope from the bag he was carrying. "Tie him up. Facedown and ass up, just like he likes it."

She rubs the palms of her hands together. "Gladly."

"Julius Withrow, addiction always comes with a price, and tonight you are in for one hell of a ride," Malakai said.

"No, no, no! You all can't do this. I know people, and I got money."

Asperilla slaps the pistol against his face. "Fuck all that shit you're talking. Get your ass on the bed," she demands.

"I'm not getting on the bed. You all will have to kill me first," Julius said.

"Kill you? Where's the fun in that? We'll make you swallow the same drugs you give your victims," Asperilla states.

"By the way, we switched your drugs while you were on your date with Trinity, but we still have your batch," Malakai said.

"Fortunately, we won't need any drugs for you. Do you know a woman named Jacquie Miller or a set of twins named Nadia and Nova? If that doesn't shift your emotions, how about a sixty-five-year-old woman named Ruth?" Malakai said.

"That's my family! Please don't hurt them," Julius cries.

"Damn, you have a whole family with the picket fence, and you out here raping women. Tsk, tsk, tsk," Asperilla says and shakes her head.

"17556 Victory Lane," Malakai mentions.

"Alright. I'll get on the bed. Please. I'm begging you. Don't hurt my family."

Julius crawls onto the bed, sniffing and wiping his tears away. "I don't deserve this. I'm sorry. I promise I won't do anything like this again."

"Get on your knees and put your arms behind your back," Trinity orders.

Trinity ties his wrists together and then his ankles. She raises his ankles over his butt and loops another knot around his ankles and wrists, bringing them together at a single point.

"Okay, he's ready," Trinity announces.

Asperilla slaps his ass cheeks. "Damn, I wish I had a dick. I want to fuck him in the ass too."

Malakai retrieves Julius' phone and turns it on. "I need you to confess to every woman you drugged and raped. I know you remember their names. If you do this, I'll leave you tied up with a virgin ass until the maid comes.

"Do we have an understanding?" Malakai asks.

Julius sniffs his nose and bobs his head yes.

Malakai instructs everyone to back away, turns on the camera, and presses record. Julius rambles off names, dates, and the type of drug he uses for his victims.

"Veronica Hemsley was the last one," Julius confesses.

Satisfied with the revelations, Malakai turns off the video. "Thank you for owning up to your addiction. Your family is safe. I don't kill kids anyway."

"So, will you all let me go now?" Julius asks.

"I got what I came for. Asperilla, he's all yours," Malakai states and walks out of the room.

"No, no, no! Don't leave me with these crazy bitches!" he screams.

"Calm down, Julius. He kept his promise. I didn't," Asperilla said. She flashes a sinister smile, retrieves a deep-throat gag, and wraps it around Julius's head.

The stainless-steel O-ring stretches Julius's mouth nice and wide.

Asperilla grabs a pillow from the bed and places it over Julius's head. "I need to know if you can take dick. That's what you tell your bitches. You better take Trinity's dick, and if you scream, I will pull this trigger and splatter your brains over these sheets."

Asperilla stands and tells Trinity he's all hers.

Trinity walks over, stroking her cock, and laughing. "Julius, get over here," she yells like the Mortal Kombat Scorpion character. "Your mouth belongs to me," she claims.

"Stick your tongue out, hoe!" Trinity yells.

Julius obeys, and she flaps her dick against his tongue.

Trinity grabs Julius's head and shoves her dick in his mouth. She feels his drool running over her dick. "I knew you like being a little bitch," Trinity said.

She ravages his mouth, pulling his head back and forth while laughing.

FLENARDO

Julius gags and Trinity pulls her dick out and spits in his mouth. "Oh baby, we're just getting started. I need to see my dick imprint inside your throat."

She starts pumping his mouth again, slapping her balls against his chin. "Julius, I want to nut in your mouth so fucking bad. Suck this dick. You're my little bitch."

She grabs his head and thrusts so hard; she catches a cramp in her butt cheeks.

"I'm catching lockjaw," he mumbles around Trinity's cock. "Can you please stop? I'm sorry for all the women I degraded and hurt," he admits.

"Okay, Julius. I'll stop."

Trinity unties the rope, and Julius's legs fall to the bed.

"Thank you. Thank you so much," he cries.

Asperilla smiles from the excitement and asks, "Julius, are you sure you don't suck dick? Because you were choking on that shit like a pro."

"Fuck y'all. A man would probably do anything when there's a gun pointed at his head."

"The gun is the least of your problems. They're okay, but I'm a razor bitch. I'll slice the tip of your dickhead off and staple it to your chest," Asperilla said.

DEVASTATION

"Julius, my pussy screams for violence. I was bored at home until we received that call. Now I'm about to catch a nut from what we do next," Asperilla, said.

"Get the oil, Trinity. Can't have your dick getting flesh burns from his tight hole," she jokes.

"No, Asperilla, please let me go," he pleads.

"When I was on the balcony, you played music to rape an innocent woman. Now it's your turn."

Asperilla logs into YouTube from her phone. "Julius, you will love this old-school song." She sings,

Hey hoe / Hey hoe

Can a nigga get some to go / Dick in your life

Asperilla gets up, waves the gun at Julius, drops low, and sings, *"you need dick in your life. What you need,* Julius. *You need dick in your life."*

She sings as Trinity squeezes the oil bottle, allowing it to run over his asshole.

Trinity takes her fingers and slides them into his asshole. She jerks her dick a few times before sliding it between his cheeks.

Once inside, she closes his legs together, gets on her knees, and slams her dick in and out of him.

"Owwww!" he yells.

Trinity grabs the pillow and presses it over his head. "Fuck you. This is my ass right now."

She plunges deep as Julius muffles words from underneath the pillow.

Trinity locks her forearms around Julius's neck and fucks him without mercy. "Take this dick, you sissy bitch. You know you love it."

Trinity squeezes her arms around Julius's neck tighter as her dick slides in and out of his asshole. "Yeah, sissy boy. I'm about to cum. Feel my power."

She yanks the pillow away from his head and presses his face into the bed. "I love your asshole, Julius. Throw it back. You know you want to."

The tension builds in Trinity, and she delivers three more hard thrusts. Pulls her dick out and nuts on Julius's back. "Aww, sissy boy. You have done well."

Julius lies flat on his face, crying and feeling sore about his manhood being snatched away.

Trinity stands up from the bed and slaps Julius's ass cheeks. "I'm going to take a piss and return to fuck you again."

Asperilla laughs and taunts Julius. "See? You shouldn't fuck with women that have friends in high places. I'll make you a deal better than the one Malakai gave you.

DEVASTATION

"We can stay here all night, and Trinity can continue fucking you in your ass or…"

"Or what? My asshole is burning. My throat is raw. Just let me go," he begs.

Asperilla stands and claps her heels together. "Okay."

She walks over and opens the balcony door. "Jump!"

"What the hell? I ain't jumping off the balcony."

"It's only two floors. Plus, there's a car below to break your fall. The worse that can happen is a broken leg. Remember, Trinity can fuck all night."

"I hate y'all's ass."

He crawls on his knees, grips the sheets for leverage, and rolls off the bed. He limps to the balcony and glances over the rail.

He turns his head back at Asperilla. "I won't forget what y'all did," Julius said.

"We won't forget what you did either," Asperilla reminds him before squeezing the trigger and watching the rounds pierce Julius's butt.

Julius skips and trips over the balcony, crashing into the car below.

"He's alive," Malakai shouts from the ground.

Asperilla blows him a kiss and screams, "I love you!"

FLENARDO

DEVASTATION

Chapter 29

One of the most critical decisions of Devin's life is finally here. He can remain in St. Louis or take his talents to a new company, and during his downtime, he can explore the best pussy Beijing has to offer.

He closes his eyes, places his head on the desk, and meditates. His body relaxes into tranquility, and he unexpectedly drifts off to sleep.

A knock at the door interrupts his peace. He taps his security app on his phone and sees Vee standing at the door with her arms folded and tapping her foot.

"Damn, I can tell she's upset about something. As a good sponsor, I better check to see what's on her mind."

He slides his chair back, jumps up, and walks through the house to invite her in.

He cracks the door open and expects a customary hug, but instead, his left cheek feels the sting from her palm.

"Devin, I hate you!" she yells.

His inner reflexes want to punch her in the chest, but he calms down and takes a deep breath.

"Vee, I have no idea what the hell you are talking about. It's best to keep your hands to yourself when you visit me."

"Speaking of visits, I had one today and am pissed. I wish I had kept my mouth shut and never mentioned Julius to you."

Devin arches his eyebrows. "Are you saying Julius stopped by your apartment today?"

"No, some detectives questioned me about the sexual assault. They asked if I would testify when everything goes to trial."

"I'm praying you told them you would testify and keep his ass locked up."

"No, I slammed the door in their faces. I'm not about to exploit my business in a courtroom."

He shakes his head and rolls his eyes. "Vee, I called in a favor to get you some justice, and now you're angry about it?"

"I didn't ask you to do anything for me!"

"Oh, I see where this is going," he implies. "Vee, please come inside. We can talk and calm down together."

"I'm not stepping foot in your house. I only came by today to inform you that I no longer need you as my sponsor or friend."

"This is bullshit, Vee, and you know it. You came over here crying your eyeballs out. What the fuck did you think was going to happen when you gave me Julius' info? Did you think I would meet him for drinks and beg him to apologize?

"That fuckboy got what he deserved. From what I was told, plenty of ladies can testify, so it's not a big deal. Just let that shit go."

"What I'm going to let go is ... your ass," she reveals.

"Once again, Vee, please come in, and let's work this out."

"And once again, Devin. I will not step foot inside your house."

"Why the hell did you come over here then?" He reaches out and grabs ahold of her arm. "Come in and stop all this shit."

She yanks her arm away from his hand, stumbles back, and falls on the floor.

He runs over to assist her, and she pushes him away.

"Get your damn hands off me! I don't need your charity," she hollers.

He balls his fists and hits the wall. "Vee, you are starting to upset me. I know you're mad about something else. What is it?

"I apologize for the detectives coming to your house. Please forgive me."

"I'm not forgiving you. Do you want people to know I'm a whore? I will show you, Ms. Shantae, and the whole class what a galactic whore looks like. I'll fuck aliens if I have to."

Devin's phone rings and startles him. "Oh shit! That dream felt scary as hell. I'll check on Vee once I finish this call."

He grabs his phone. "Hello."

"Mr. Williams, your time is up. I need an answer immediately."

He slides his chair back from the desk and spins around in a circle as he thinks deeply about his future with the new company.

The chair stops twirling, and he stands up and walks to his window. "Ms. Yu Yan, my answer is yes."

"Thank you for the prompt reply. I'll be in touch this week with all the necessary documents."

Ms. Yu Yan disconnects the call without saying another word.

"She didn't say goodbye or Zàijiàn in her host language," he muses.

DEVASTATION

He stares out the window and admires the flashing lights reflecting from the poles on the dual sides of the St. Louis Arch.

He turns around and dials Vee's number as he returns to his desk. Her phone goes to voicemail. Since he hasn't heard from her in two days, he visits her apartment.

He locates the nearest Uber driver, gathers his things, and walks downstairs to catch his ride.

The driver pulls up to the curb and rolls down her window. "Wow, you are very handsome," she compliments.

He smiles back at her and says, "I can tell this will be a fun ride."

She turns on the music and sings as she drives Devin to his destination.

Devin inhales her perfume. "Your insatiable scent is lingering its way to the back seat."

"Why, thank you, Mr. Handsome."

They chat and flirt until they reach Vee's apartment. Devin steps out of the car and smiles at the driver again. "What's your name?"

"Aaliyah," she responds.

"Beautiful name. I'm going to give you five stars plus a great tip."

FLENARDO

He waves goodbye to Aaliyah, turns around, and walks to Vee's apartment building.

He knocks on her door and waits for someone to come and let him in. He remains still for a few more minutes before knocking harder. The door creeps open, and he pushes the door and walks in.

Joe runs up and jumps on him. He pats Joe's head. "What's going on, Joe Joe? Where's your funky ass mama at?"

He overhears the music from the bedroom and prays Vee's not drunk or high.

He cracks the door open and peeps in, catching Vee's reflection in the mirror, being fuck doggystyle by a stranger. The image brings flashbacks of rage built inside from his days with Simone.

He pushes the door hard, and the back of the doorknob slams against the wall. "You were raped two weeks ago, and you're already fucking random strangers!

"I'm glad I'm taking the job in Beijing!" he angrily shouts as he turns and steps out of the bedroom.

The unknown stranger scrambles to find his clothes while Vee jumps up, grabs a T-shirt, and runs after Devin.

Devin makes his way to the front door. Vee yells, "wait," before he steps outside.

"There's nothing more you can say. I'm unsure why I'm making such a big deal about this. We are whores, so you can fuck whomever you choose."

"Devin, that's not fair. My itch kicked in. I couldn't focus, and the toys weren't working. Sorry for letting you down, but I needed some dick."

"Well, I'm sure you have plenty of dick in the bedroom to scratch that itch," he reminds her sarcastically.

"Vee, it's okay. I'm tired of being drained by our friend/relationship.

"I am addicted to buying pussy, and if I were set up and robbed, even I would be hesitant to jump back in the game.

"You know it's too early to be fucking people off the internet."

"Says who? Who made you captain of the pussy patrol?"

"Vee, you sound dumb as fuck. Listen and listen well. Our sponsorship is over. You are free to fuck whomever, whenever, however, and wherever the fuck you want."

"Fine. I will!" she yells.

Devin walks out the door without looking back, wishing he never came to check on Vee.

FLENARDO

DEVASTATION

Chapter 30

Devin stands butt naked and with a stiff dick in front of his full-length mirror. His chest rises and falls from his heavy breathing. The veins in his arms are bursting through his skin, and tears are sliding down his face as he re-experiences the disgusting image of Vee fucking that guy.

He despises himself for trying to save her, but most of all, the man staring back at him in the mirror is disgusting.

He snatches the scissors from the dresser, grabs a hand full of locs, and starts cutting. The locs tumbles along his shoulders and onto the floor.

He snatches more of his locs and screams, "I hate my fucking life!"

He keeps cutting and shouting until his hair looks like a chia pet on top of his head.

He walks to the bathroom and searches for his clippers. He will return to his original signature temp fade haircut for the first time in eight years.

He smiles in the mirror as he cuts off his hair. He's thrilled to be flying to Beijing with a new style and willing to practice abstinence once he arrives in China.

FLENARDO

He edges the hairline across his forehead, sits the clippers down, and steps back.

"There you go. It has been a long time since I have seen this version of myself. No drama, no cheating fiancé, and now I'll have more money for other things instead of buying pussy."

He sweeps the hair from the floor and tosses it in the trash. His mind swings back to Vee. "No, that energy is toxic. I need a distraction."

He grabs his phone and calls Armocita. His dick swells as he anticipates her sweet voice saying, 'hey, baby.'

She answers, and like clockwork, she responds in his favorite greeting.

He smiles and waits a few seconds. "Good evening, Ms. Exquisite. I hope your day was fulfilling."

"My day was incredible and successful. The only thing I need now is for you to tuck me in for tonight."

"Oh really? Would you like a bedtime story as well?"

"Yes, I would love a story, but only if you speak softly between my thighs."

"Sounds tempting. I have a surprise for you tonight, so I'll see you once I shower and get dressed."

"I can't wait and don't forget to bring a bottle of wine. I drank what was left of mine last night."

"No worries. I got you covered. See you soon."

He ends the call and thinks abstinence can wait one more day. He sings and dances on his way to the shower. He needs this moment of rejuvenation and the taste of Armocita sweet-smelling nectars.

After his revitalizing shower, he dries his body and calls the parking garage attendant. "George, tonight I'm ready."

"Devin, you have to be shitting me. You haven't driven that car in over five years."

"I know, but I'm feeling different and not in the mood for an Uber. Plus, it will be the last time I drive it."

"Why is that?"

"Because I'm giving the car to you."

"What the fuck?"

"No bullshit, George. It's yours after tonight."

"So, you are giving me a fully loaded Scat Pack with less than five thousand miles on it?"

"You washed it monthly and drove it down the highway to blow the cobwebs off. It's the least I can do."

"Thanks, Devin. I mean it. I promised to take good care of it."

"I know you will. Go ahead and pull it around. I'll be down in a minute."

Devin hangs up the phone, snaps a motivational photo of Devastation, and sends it to Armocita with the caption, 'open wide.'

He finds and puts on an outfit and shoes, locks the door, and rides the elevator down to the lobby.

As he steps outside the building, George accelerates the gas, and the Scat Pack engine roars, startling and capturing the pedestrians' attention.

George steps out of the car and tosses Devin the key. "Make sure you return my future vehicle in one piece."

Devin hugs George. "No worries. The car will be returned like it's brand new, and you can race it down the interstate."

Devin turns around, sits in the driver's seat, and zooms down the road, leaving tire tracks and smoke as he speeds to see Armocita.

He arrives at Armocita's complex, parks his car, and calls her while walking to her door.

"Shit! I forgot the wine," he remembers, as the phone rings in his ear.

She answers, and he quickly babbles about forgetting to stop at the store because he was ecstatic to drive his car and see her.

DEVASTATION

"Devin, fuck the wine. Just get in here and slay me with Devastation. My pussy lips have been quivering nonstop since I ate those edibles."

"Don't worry. I'm on my way."

He hangs up the phone and runs the rest of the way. He arrives at her door and pounds his fist against it. "Armocita, hurry up!" he screams.

She opens her door, places her hands over her mouth, and stares at Devin's new look.

She rubs her hand over his head. "I can't believe you cut your hair. It will take a minute to grow on me, but you are still sexy as fuck."

He looks down and whispers, "Armocita," while pointing at her short velvet robe.

"Oh shit! I forgot I answered the door with my robe open. I'm showing the world this spellbinding pussy."

"Titties, too," he admires and praises.

She closes her robe and drags him inside her apartment.

"This is what I get for eating edibles and trying to get fucked."

"Oh, you will still get that," he assures her and grins.

He walks over, wraps his hands around her upper thighs, and lifts her onto his shoulders as her robe swings open.

"Dammit, Devin. I can't pull your locs this time," she complains.

"Pull my fucking ears. Because I'm going in," he claims.

He inhales her aroma, hovers over her clit, and wraps his mouth around it, slowly lapping and curling his tongue instantaneously.

He pulls his mouth back slightly and plunges back in.

She wraps her hands around his head and grinds her pussy in his face.

He eats her pussy, walking and peeping out the side of his eye as he travels to her bedroom.

He gently lies her on the bed, repositions her on his face, and feasts on her juices. He slaps her ass cheeks and bites the tip of her clit.

She reaches one hand back and plays with his hard dick through his pants. "Umm, I needed this," she moans.

He squeezes her nipples with his fingertips while chewing on her clit with his teeth.

"Oh shit, baby. Please do it again!" she cries.

She sways her waist, and her pussy slides to his forehead and back down to his chin. "Eat this pussy. Put your tongue through my walls."

He lifts her from the bed, spins around, and lies Armocita on her back. She throws her legs in the air, and he kisses the back of her knees, thighs, and ass cheeks.

She bends her knees back. He opens her pussy lips and slurps and smacks on her juices.

She places her foot on his shoulder and curves the other leg ninety degrees on the bed. She grabs his head and smears his face deeper into her abyss.

She closes her eyes and embraces the orgasm that is soon to come.

He sucks and pulls on her lips. She moans and moans deeper.

He lifts his chin and runs his tongue from her lips to her asshole. He repeats the motions as she places the pillow on her face.

He tugs on her lips and jabs his tongue inside of her.

She throws the pillow on the floor and screams, "you better make me cum! Make me cum now!"

She lifts her legs in the air. She wraps her arm around one of her thighs and grabs Devin's head with her other hand.

His neck tilts and bobs like a chicken as he eats her pussy faster.

She moans intensively as her toes begin to curl. "Oh shit! I'm about to cum. That's the spot. Keep sucking, muthafucker."

The bed bounces up and down as he whacks his face against her wet pussy repeatedly.

"Mmm… Mmm," she wails.

Devin tastes her essence as it runs down his throat. She squirts heavily enough to make him gag.

He grips her thighs, holds on, and swallows everything she's got because there's no telling when he'll taste pussy again.

She exhales, and her legs descend back to bed. "Thank you," she whispers.

He slides from the bed, strips out his clothes, and strokes his dick in front of her. "My turn," he reminds her.

He walks over, and her mouth welcomes his inches as she plays with his nutsack.

He fucks her throat while she winks her left eye back at him.

Damn, I'm going to miss this mouth, he thinks.

He slides his dick from her glory hole and flips Armocita onto her stomach. She braces her body with her elbows and knees as Devin places his hands on her shoulder and enters her from behind.

DEVASTATION

"How bad do you want your pussy devastated?"

"To the max," she replies.

He smashes his dick in as she grips the sheets. Her ass cheeks smack loudly and rhythmically against his pelvis.

He leans over, jerks her head back by her throat, and kisses her forehead. "Bitch, I'm going to destroy you."

He pushes her face into the bed, closes her legs, and arches over her back.

He fucks her rough as she moans. His dick digs deeper, and her ass cheek muscles jiggle from every stroke.

He falls on her and pounds her while she yells, "fuck me, Devin."

He increases his strokes and pulls her hair. "Make me cum in this pussy. Be my nasty bitch one last time."

He lifts her head back and kisses her on the mouth as she squirms and attempts to escape the dick.

He flips her over and folds her legs and knees up by her head. He jumps back in her pussy, and his hips and muscles flex and tighten as he thrusts harder.

"Fuck. I'm going to cum in your pussy tonight."

His dick slides out, and he pushes it right back in. His balls are beating against her ass cheeks and drowning out her cries for help.

FLENARDO

He feels his nut rising. He grunts and pumps and screams. "I'm about to cum!"

His strokes move like waves crashing against the shores. He delivers a few more blows and feels a bolt of electricity shooting through his dick and erupting through Armocita's wet pussy.

He continues his strokes while cumming, and she screams, "oh my God, I love you!"

He slides out of her pussy slowly, breathing heavily, and lies beside her.

Armocita lies expressionless, staring at the ceiling and not saying a word.

"I need you to listen for a moment," he asserts.

"I will destroy your mouth, pussy, and asshole tonight. I will eat all the pain I will deliver and cripple you again.

"After tonight, you will be the last piece of pussy I buy. I'm starting my new career in Beijing.

"In the morning, you will have enough money in your bank account to live comfortably for the next five years and purchase your fitness building, so you no longer have to rent.

"I will miss you, but I need to do better with my life, and you need a man that will cherish and reverence you.

DEVASTATION

You are intelligent, and please know your worth before settling and sleeping with anyone.

"I'm sure you will be married and have beautiful kids the next time I see you."

She turns her head and stares into his eyes. She senses his pain, grabs his head, and cuddles it on her chest.

"Thank you for everything," she whispers.

He lifts his head from her chest and slides down between her thighs. "Tell me about your future dreams. I won't stop eating until I've heard them all."

"I'm going to make up some goals so you can stay down there all night," she jokes.

"Do whatever you like," he whispers, kissing her inner thighs.

While Devin tastes his leftover cream and her juices, she starts talking about her visions.

FLENARDO

DEVASTATION

Chapter 31

Vee struggles to open her eyelids, and her head is pounding from a severe migraine.

She only remembers popping ecstasy pills and drinking whiskey and vodka last night.

She has no idea how she ended up naked and lying on her stomach on the living room floor.

She rolls over and notices the dried-up cum splatter on her thighs and breasts. "Eww, this shit is nasty."

She scoots toward the round coffee table, presses her hands on the top, and lifts herself from the ground.

A sharp pain shoots through her lower back as she stands up. She drags her feet as she walks toward the bathroom.

She hears Joe barking from inside the bathroom. "What the hell is he doing in there instead of his bed?"

She opens the door, and he runs out, jumps in the air, and places his paws on her thighs.

"Okay, Joe. I love you too. Please go to bed while I shower."

She leads him to the bedroom, opens the door, and finds two guys unconscious on her bed. Joe barks in rage as Vee screams, "get the fuck out!"

The guys don't budge a muscle. Vee leaves the bedroom and stomps into the kitchen. She finds a pot under the cabinet and fills it with cold water.

She marches back to the room, tosses the water over the bed, and it lands on their naked skin. "I said, get the fuck out!"

The guys jump from the bed and bump their heads against each other.

She leaves the bedroom and returns with her pistol pointing at the guys. "How the fuck are you all going to sleep in my bed and leave me on the floor?

"Inconsiderate assholes. Get your shit and get the fuck out of my house right now before I start shooting," she threatens them while keeping her finger on the trigger.

They scramble to find their clothes while Vee steps to the side, allowing them to rush out of the bedroom. She follows them as they run out the door in underwear and socks.

Vee locks the door behind them and hurries to the shower. She turns on the water and prepares to wash away last night's episode.

DEVASTATION

She has been meeting random guys at the bar for the past few days and inviting them to an 'after-party.' She never remembers the details during those nights nor the violations they do to her body.

She opens her medicine cabinet, swallows two Sumatriptan tablets, and steps in the shower.

She stands under the hot water scratching her skin, hoping to remove the leftover sex scent and men's cologne.

Fucking random strangers has become her routine, and the shower is her confessional booth.

"Why can't I stop being a cum-dumpster?" she asks herself.

She leans against the shower wall and cries before she reaches for a washcloth and continues her whoremonger cleansings.

After being satisfied with scrubbing and rinsing her body repeatedly, she turns off the water, wraps a towel around herself, and finds a funny cartoon print onesie to wear.

She snatches the sheets, pillowcases, and comforter off the bed. "Guess I'll have to throw these away now. I'm not sleeping on these ever again."

Joe follows her out the back door as she throws her third comforter set away in the dumpster.

FLENARDO

She waits while Joe takes a piss and shit in Michael's yard. Watching Joe have fun creates a moment of happiness before she heads back into her gloomy residence.

Once inside, she feeds Joe, pickups up her diary, and flops on the sofa.

Nympho Log: 6 May 2022

It has been a while since I have written inside of you. If I stroke my pen more across these pages, I could free myself from dick.

This past month has been interesting. One minute I was great friends with Devin; the next, I was his mortal enemy. I'm not sure if our relationship will heal this time.

Allow me to explain. I was raped by Julius but was too afraid of people judging my sex life to testify.

I shouldn't have fucked a guy so soon after my trauma, but the itch was too much. I attempted DIY projects, read novels, and even went to church.

Toys weren't working and watching porn didn't help the situation either. Once, I handcuffed myself to the bed and drank alcohol until I passed out. That lasted for one night, and the itch came back even worse. It seemed like the itch knew I was trying to fight against it.

I'm weak and know I will hate myself every morning after my asinine behavior.

DEVASTATION

Diary, I think that's all I have for today. Thanks for not judging me; I will have better news to share one day.

Keep the pages wet, and I'll stroke you another time.

Love, Veronica Marie Hemsley.

Nympho out.

She closes the diary and says, " Hey Siri, Call Devin on speakerphone."

The phone rings and rings, but Devin never answers.

She grabs her phone and ends the call.

"Why does he act this way? He's in the class too and should understand the life of a hoe. I have never complained or judged him for spending his money on pussy."

She stands from the sofa, bites her nails, and contemplates what she can do besides riding someone's son's dick.

She grabs her phone again and texts, *can you please come over to my apartment so that I won't do anything wild today?* to Ms. Shantae.

She waits on her response, and the sex demon in her head whispers, *go to the bar again and flirt with more guys.*

Ms. Shantae replied and asked Vee to come to her house instead. She texted her the address and said she could come over around five.

Vee balls her fists, raises her arm, and pulls it down to celebrate. "Yes!" she shouts.

She has dodged a bullet tonight and prays Ms. Shantae can guide her away from her struggles.

She wishes Devin was around to console her and misses their Criminal Minds dates.

She refuses to give up on Devin and decides to call him again; the results are still the same.

She shrugs her shoulder and goes into the bedroom to find something comfortable to wear for today.

She decides to go thrift shopping, and maybe Kaylene will be free to hang out with her until she meets Ms. Shantae.

DEVASTATION

Chapter 32

Devin leans over his balcony, sips his green tea, and observes the morning people scurrying around like ants to their destination.

He has no regrets about taking the job, and his most accomplished goal thus far is ignoring the lust for the flesh for an entire month. To him, that's infinity times twelve.

Now and then, he thinks of Vee and prays she is finding her purpose in life.

During his last video session with Ms. Shantae, he was tempted to ask about Vee, but he figured letting sleeping dogs lie in their shit would be better.

The doorbell rings, and he hears keys jingling in the lock. He checks the time and knows he will have to talk Devastation from thumping and bursting through his honeycomb yellow sating pajama pants.

He hears the voices of two Chinese women talking and preparing to clean up the apartment.

These women do everything except wash his dick. The first night he arrived, they ran his water, and refused to leave the bathroom.

Luckily, he knew a few Chinese words to tell them he could scrub his own balls.

"Zǎo shàng hǎo, dé wén," they announce as they approach the balcony.

He loves how his name rolls off their tongue as they deliver the morning greeting.

He knows how to say beautiful in Chinese, so he turns around and says, "Morning, měi lì."

They giggle, slap his ass, and tidy up the apartment.

He is cautious when conversing on the phone if they are around. He keeps his communication with the ladies brief, sometimes funny, but always professional.

He walks past them to his bedroom and turns on some music to get dressed for his first day of work.

Ms. Yu Yan gave him time to acclimate to the culture, but she warned him the average Chinese software technician would run circles around America's most prestigious worker.

Devin desires a challenge and can't wait to go to work and demonstrate why losing is not a part of his DNA.

He steps into his walk-in closet and notices his shoes are shining and the suits are pressed. He will have to tip the housemaids extra before he departs.

DEVASTATION

"Suit or jeans," he ponders as he slides the hangers across the rails.

"Ms. Yu Yan never told me what to wear. Should I show up as a businessman or a relaxed technician?"

He snaps his finger. "Got it."

He grabs his phone, searches for Google Translate, and starts a dialogue with the sexy housekeepers.

He enters the living room and catches the ladies dancing to Beyonce's video.

He types in the phrase, 'excuses me, but what does an average person where to a big corporation?'

He presses translate and raises the phone so that the ladies can hear.

They laugh and whisper some Chinese dialogue to each other.

"Ladies, this is serious. Come in the bedroom and help a black man out this morning."

They follow him back into the bedroom, and the first housekeeper pulls out an outfit and shows it to the other woman.

The housekeeper outside the closet shakes her head from side to side, disapproving of the outfit.

They continue flashing outfits until the housekeeper finds a long-sleeved white shirt and matches it with a button-down vest, khakis, and a pair of crisp white shoes.

The second housekeeper tugs on his pajamas' waistband. "Take off your pants," she demands.

He steps back from her grasp and stumbles on the bed.

They giggle again before taking charge of the situation. They picked out his watch and recommended his cologne to go with his clothes for today.

Once his makeover is complete, he walks to the mirror and smiles.

"Thank you, ladies. I can get used to this. You all can dress me every day."

They giggle and whisper to each other as they walk out of the bedroom and back to the living room to watch more music videos.

He places his work computer in his bag, grabs his phone, and strolls out of the bedroom.

He stops and waves at the housekeepers. He crosses his arms over his shoulder, demonstrating a hug.

They understand his technique and come over and hug him.

He kisses each lady on the cheeks and slaps their ass before walking out the door.

DEVASTATION

I can't fuck them, but that doesn't mean I cannot flirt when they come over, he thinks to himself.

To stay in shape, he usually walks down twenty-four flights of stairs. He doesn't mind the walk, and with the elevator stopping at every floor, he can avoid the morning crowd and reach the lobby before all of the other tenants.

He greets the doorman and walks one mile to his new job. The crowd is shoulder to shoulder, with most of them heading to the subway for their daily commute.

Thank God my job is close to my condo, he thinks, as he continues his walk.

He arrives at the job and flashes his CAC card to the security officer.

The officer scans the card and checks the picture with the face. "Okay. Follow me, and I'll lead you to your new office."

The work floor atmosphere differs from St. Louis, with no music or people joking. All you hear is keys pecking and paper printing.

The security officer points to the office door, and Devin smiles when he sees his name on the plaque.

"Thank you," he responds to the security guard and sets up his computer and office.

When he powers up his laptop and opens Microsoft Word, his folders update, and emails populate. Most of them are from Ms. Yu Yan.

He looks over the monitor and sees an attractive Chinese woman with thick hips staring at him.

"Hello, can I help you?" he asks.

"Please speak English," he mumbles under his breath.

"Morning, I'm Ling, Ms. Yu Yan's secretary," she introduces herself and walks over to shake his hand.

They shake hands, and then Ling pulls her hand back. "Ms. Yu Yan is ready to see you now. By the way, welcome to Beijing."

He follows behind her and watches as her butt jiggles up and down as she leads him into Ms. Yu Yan's office.

"Step in and closes the door," Ms. Yu Yan orders.

"How are you enjoying your time here? Have you allowed the housekeepers to clean your chimney yet?"

"I wasn't aware the condominium came with a chimney."

"Devin, stop being so humorless. I was speaking about them cleaning your asshole," she jokes.

"Oh, my bad. I think I will pass on that maintenance inspection. Plus, I have decided to go the abstinent route for the moment."

"Impressive. It appears a lot has changed since the banquet in St. Louis. Feel free to explore if you decide to cash in the chimney experience."

"Thanks, but no thanks," he answers. "Ms.Yu-"

"Diana," she interrupts. "Call me Diana."

"Okay, Diana. What can I do for you and your lovely company today?"

"At the end of the week, a competition will be between my top engineer and yourself. I need to see how good you are," she informs him, sliding over a secret file.

"Devin, I didn't bring you here for your skills in building client portfolios and start-up companies. You have some unique hacking skills that could be very valuable to my friends and me," she states.

"It looks like you know another one of my secrets. I better upgrade my firewall," he comments.

"It looks that way," she responds.

She stands from her seat, walks over, and kisses his cheeks. She trails her mouth to his earlobe and whispers, "don't let me down, or you'll regret it.

"Now get out of my office and get to work," she instructs.

FLENARDO

DEVASTATION

Chapter 33

Vee points her index finger in the air, indicating the bartender to bring her another glass filled with Smirnoff Red, White, and Berry Vodka.

She sits in her favorite bar top chair, singing along to a song from the speakers and scanning the room for some dick.

She repeats the last conversation with Ms. Shantae in her mind. *Devin left, and this rehab isn't the same without him. I pushed him away, and he's better off without a stupid bitch like me. Ms. Shantae, I'm going to fuck my brains out now. Just answer my calls when I need to vent.*

She sighs deeply, shakes her head, and drowns her sorrows with the vodka. She burps and clings the bottom of the glass on the counter. "One more, Mr. Bartender. Bring a bitch one more."

She spins around in the bar seat and scans the room again while the bartender fixes her fifth drink.

She rolls her eyes and smiles at the white male across the room but is not in the mood for vanilla tonight.

She looks again, and her prize is at the pool table. "Bingo!" she shouts.

There, standing six-foot tall, was a sexy Cuban-African man with short wavy hair, a pearly white smile, and hypnotizing eyes, wearing a two-piece gray vest and slacks ensemble.

His shirt sleeves roll up to his elbows, and his biceps muscles are stiff and flexing.

He glides the pool stick back and forward, tapping the white ball.

Vee watches as the ball connects with the number two ball and falls into the corner pocket.

She imagines the pool stick transforming into a dick and his balls dropping in her mouth instead of the pocket.

She spins around to retrieve her drink from the bartender. She takes a sip, gets up from her seat, and walks over to this gentleman who reminds her of Laz Alonso.

She pushes out her chest and showcases her thirty-eight G's as she steps into his space.

"Can you teach me how to hold the stick?" she asks as she continues to flirt by rolling her tongue over the tip of the straw.

"It depends on if your hands can hold a tight grip. I can't play with women with sweaty hands. It's easy to drop the stick, and that's a no-go for this game."

She sits her drink on the table's ledge and snatches the stick from his hands.

She leans over, her red and black skirt fans up, and he sees her thick thighs and tattoos through her see-through stockings.

She retracts the stick and releases it like the handle of a pinball machine. The white ball misses every ball on the table and lunges into the bottom corner pocket.

"Shit, I guess these aren't the balls I should be playing with tonight," she jokes.

"Maybe not. I didn't catch your name."

"I didn't give it, but you can call me Bathroom Becky tonight."

He laughs and retrieves his stick from her hand. "You are a freaky bitch. I like that, and I'm long overdue for a release."

She wraps her fingers around the flap of his collar shirt. "Follow me to the women's bathroom, and let's flush something out."

She steps away, and he throws the stick on the table. He looks around the room, but no one is paying attention.

He runs behind her, wraps his arms around her waist, and kisses her right ear lobe.

She pushes the bathroom door open, walks in, and kicks in the stall with her boot.

She grabs his shirt, yanks him in, and makes him sit on the toilet.

She hikes her skirt up, rips her stocking, and sticks her fingers in her opening pussy. She circles her walls, pulls them out, and rubs her fingers from his forehead to his lips.

"You like the way my pussy smells?" she asks.

"Hell yeah," he responds.

He unbuckles his pants and pulls them down to his ankles.

She straddles him, grabs his dick, and slides it in her pussy. She starts slowly, lifts her waist, and glides it down.

He palms the back of her ass, cups the lower section of her ass cheeks, and assists her as she rides his dick.

"Ooh, shit," she moans.

"You like that, Becky? You better ride my dick."

He slides his hips back against the toilet and rams his dick inside as she rides down.

"I'm playing pool in your pussy now," he mentions while jabbing her right and left corner pockets.

"Oh yeah, play it, daddy. Knock all my corners!" she shouts.

She leans forward and rides him faster, clinching his dick with her Kegel's muscles.

His face tenses and drool runs down the side of his jaw. He lifts his palm off her ass and wipes his face.

"Becky, I love the way you ride this dick. I'm going to bust this nut in a few minutes."

She smiles and places two fingers over his mouth. "Hush," she whispers. "You're not exploding in me. I have the perfect home for your trick shot. This fuck session is a pool game," she reminds him and continues bouncing on his dick.

She lifts her hips, slides away from his dick, and turns around. She bends over, grabs her ankles, and plops down on his dick.

She squeezes her ankles tighter and slams harder on his dick.

The two skull tattoos on each of her ass cheeks captivate his mind. He pictures the skulls opening their mouth and welcoming him to hell's gates every time she recoils off his lap.

He takes his hands, spread her ass cheeks open, and watches her pussy lips dance on his pole.

"Becky, I'm about to cum."

She springs from his lap, drops to her knees, and uses her mouth like a vacuum cleaner. She deepthroats his dick down to his balls and releases her mouth after passing the head.

She hums on his balls and jerks his dick up and down with her hands. She spits and licks saliva off his mushroom tip.

She looks up and asks, "are you ready to shoot your nut in the corner or deep in my mouth?"

"I'll shoot anywhere you desire," he answers.

She swirls her tongue over his head and gobbles her mouth down on his shaft. She comes up and licks the sides of his dick before returning to her prize.

He grabs the back of her head and pushes her face forward while obliterating her mouth. "Yes, baby, suck this dick. This is the head game you wanted to play. Suck on this pool stick. You better not make me miss."

She becomes turned on by his commands and sucks harder. Her spits run from her mouth and along his dick. There's a thick glob dripping and forming a miniature waterfall, ready to run over onto the floor.

She whips her head forward and downward, grips her fist tighter, and squeezes his dick.

DEVASTATION

He shifts from the toilet and stands on his feet. He grabs the side of the stall walls with both hands.

"Yeah, Becky, you about to win this game," he grunts.

The stall door shakes and rattles the hinges as he fucks her mouth. His hands tremble, and his booty cheeks tighten as he prepares for one of the biggest nuts he has ever experienced.

"Ooh. Ooh. Here it comes."

His nut blazes through his dick like an Olympic runner, and her mouth is the finish line.

She anticipates and sucks his dick harder. She moans as the hot cum stimulates her tongue. She gulps his seeds down her throat.

"Mmm. Mmm," she moans.

He exhales as the built-up stress disappears from his body. His limp dick falls out her mouth as he sits on the toilet.

"Great game. Eight ball, corner pocket," he announces.

She stands to her feet and wipes her mouth. "Yeah, my mouth never loses."

"Cut!" the director yells from outside the bathroom stall.

FLENARDO

The director walks over and pats Vee on the back. "Great job, Bathroom Becky. The next scene is a threesome with a little person and a seven-footer. Are you ready?"

"Yes, get me some more drinks and an edible."

She sings a verse from a Prince song,

Baby I'm a star

Might not know it now

Baby but I are, I'm a star

I don't won't to stop, 'til I reach the top

Sing it. We are all a star!

DEVASTATION

Chapter 34

Vee places her thumb in her mouth, bites off the nail, and spits it across the exam room floor.

She looks across the room, and her face cringes. "Ugh, all these safe sex books and abstinence posters.

"I initially informed him that protection is my number one rule. I wish the dick was lousy for once, but his stroke game came from Krypton. I had no idea he was fucking me raw from the back. I saw him open the condom and put it on.

"Nut was dripping out my pussy and slowly sliding down my inner thighs.

"I can't trust any of these muthafuckers these days."

She scrolls to her Tinder profile and looks for more dick until the doctor returns with her results. She might have syphilis, chlamydia, gonorrhea, or trichomoniasis and can't have sex for a while.

The good news is she can fuck as soon as she leaves the clinic if everything comes back clean.

She slaps her hand against her thigh while looking at her phone. "Damn, this guy is fine as hell. Please have my pussy come back clean," she prays.

She looks through his other photos and checks his relationship status. She was moments away from sliding down her top and texting him a tit pic before she heard the doctor's voice outside the door.

She straightens her shirt and attempts to act normal as the doctor knocks on the door and enters the room.

"Okay, Veronica, your results came back, and you might as well stand to your feet and start clapping."

She smiles at the doctor, leaps off the table, claps, and dances around the room.

The doctor erupts with laughter and snorts through her nose while holding her stomach.

"Yes, that's right. Put those hands together. Congratulations, you have The Clap. Three cheers for Veronica Hemsley!" she shouts.

"Hilarious, Dr. Armstrong. You got me excited for nothing."

"Better to laugh than to die. I have been treating you for the past ten years, and you are still doing the same thing repeatedly.

DEVASTATION

"The results could have been worse. You could have contracted HIV or full-blown AIDS.

"I will prescribe you some Doxycycline, and you need to abstain from sex until I see you again in about ten days.

"You will need to contact your last few partners and inform them of your results," she recommends.

"Bullshit," she muzzles with a fake cough.

"I'm serious, Veronica. Call as many as you can remember."

"Did you call Ms. Shantae, too?" Vee asks.

"As soon as you walked in the door. She will expect you to stop by this week."

She walks over and hugs Dr. Armstrong. "One day, I will come here as a new woman."

"Lord, I hope so. All it takes is the wrong pole in the right hole, and there goes your soul," she rhymes.

Vee shakes her head. "I'll keep that thought in the back of my head." She grabs her prescriptions and pamphlets and walks out the door.

She enters the lobby with her head held high and passes all the judgmental people without giving them a second look.

She walks to her car, opens the door, and sits in the driver's seat. She pulls out her phone and stares at the sexy guy from earlier. She snaps a photo of her tit and sends it to him with the captions; *I'll give you more than this in about two weeks.*

He sends back a thumbs-up emoji.

"Thumbs-up? What the fuck? My pretty areole with the nipple ring is worth more than a thumbs-up. What a dick!"

She deletes his profile, attaches her phone to the dash mount, and rides home to take Joe to the park.

"Since I can't fuck, I'll find a book to read and throw the doggie toys with my baby."

She listens to the radio, speeds through traffic, and updates alerts for other drivers on her police GPS tracker.

She arrives in her parking lot in less than thirty minutes, slides out of the car, and walks across the grass.

She hears Joe barking and scratching the door as she approaches it.

She turns the key in the lock and opens the door. Joe zooms by her legs, run to the tree, and returns to the porch.

He jumps on her leg and dashes back to the tree.

He trots in a circle while sniffing for a recognizable scent.

She stands with her hands on her hip and yells, "hurry up and stop playing!"

He barks at her.

DEVASTATION

"Hey, no backtalk! Just pee and come on," Vee demands.

He lifts his hind leg and pisses a long yellowish stream at the bottom of the tree.

He shakes his left leg, releases the last few drips, and kicks grass with his back legs.

He runs into the house, and she gives him a treat.

She enters her bedroom to grab her iPad and returns to the living room. "Ok, Joe, you ready for a ride?"

He jumps up, barking and wagging his little nub.

She locks her door, and Joe follows her to the car. "Mommy's taking you to the park. Up. Up," she commands.

Joe squats down and jumps in the passenger seat.

She walks to the driver's side, gets in, slides on her shades, and cruises to the park.

On her way there, she calls Kaylene and explains her STD drama. In moments like this, she misses Devin, but her pussy is a demon. It destroyed their friendship because it needed a dick to stay alive.

Kaylene becomes a mother figure and preaches to Vee about her sex life.

Vee hears some of what she is saying, and the truth irritates her, so she makes an excuse to get off the phone.

She promises to call her back after she enjoys the park with Joe and reads some mind-blowing smut.

She arrives at the park, pops her trunk, and pulls out the basket of toys and a blanket.

She finds a nice quiet spot, kneels, and spreads the blanket on the grass. She rolls Joe's toys out, lies on her stomach, and retrieves her iPad.

Joe clamps his teeth on one of the toys and shakes it while it's in his mouth.

She turns on her iPad and finds a new series by BD Hampton. She loves his BWWM nasty novellas, and today's reading is titled *My Hot Black Stepmom*.

She reads the synopsis and discovers Ben is an eighteen-year-old virgin fantasizing about fucking his stepmother.

"Oh shit, I know this is going to be good."

She flings the ball through the air and watches Joe race to retrieve it.

She scrolls her finger across the iPad and laughs from reading about Ben being embarrassed about having a hard-on and taking off running once his stepmother sees it.

DEVASTATION

Chapter 35

The clacking of keyboard keys echoes across the room, and neither competitor looks at the other while hacking into the website.

Devin taps the enter key and installs the malicious code. He leans back in his chair and blows an air kiss to Ms. Yu Yan as she watches him from outside the glass screen.

Ms. Yu Yan whispers to another woman, "he's an egotistical asshole, but we need him."

She presses a red button below the window, and the room door opens for them to exit.

Devin stands and shakes hands with the gentlemen. "You gave me a run for my money, and I can't wait until our next challenge."

Devin walks out of the room and shouts, "Fánróng!"

He runs over to Ms. Yu Yan and squeezes the side of her hips, lifting her from the ground and spinning her around.

He places her back on the floor. "Did I say the word boom correctly in Chinese?" he asks.

"You did ok for an American but don't pick me up in front of my staff again."

"I apologize. I got excited and carried away. It won't happen again," he explains.

"I know because the next time it does, your ass will be terminated," she informs.

"Now go home and relax. I'll be in touch when I need you again."

Devin shrugs his shoulder and decides not to ask why she was excusing him from work.

Probably because I made a mockery of their top engineer, he thinks while gathering his things from his cubicle.

On his way out, he stops at the secretary's desk.

"Can you recommend a place where I can drink and admire the city's finest women?" he asks.

She places the pen tip on the corner of her mouth and crosses her right ankle over her left foot. "Umm, you don't look like the Suzie Wong cosplay type. Maybe you should try Club Mix. It has an American feel with hip-hop, and the atmosphere is crazy."

"Modern hip-hop isn't my thing, and that place sounds like something for the younger generation.

"What else can you offer me, or do I need to ask Ms. Yu Yan?"

"I thought American men loved hip-hop and quickie sex with Chinese women."

"Sometimes, but recommend something upscale for me," he proposes.

"Okay, why don't you try *Guŏzhī*?"

"Did you say coochie?" he asks.

"No, *Guŏzhī*," she enunciates again.

"Well, the Chinese expression of that word sounds like the word coochie."

"Another thing, it's not a place to go alone," she advises.

"Thanks for the tip. I'm sure I can find someone to accompany me tonight."

He notices her squinting eyes widen, and a cool-scented breath of air blows behind his neck.

"Devin Williams, go home and stop harassing my secretary."

"I promise I'm leaving. Just trying to find a place to relax as you suggested. Tonight, I'm going to a place that sounds like the word coochie."

"*Guŏzhī*," she pronounces.

"Yes, that's the place."

"Well, why are you still standing here?" Ms. Yu Yan asks. "Leave and take your two housekeepers with you. You will need a woman or two to enter the club."

He nods his head. "Enjoy your weekend, and I'll see you Monday," he proclaims.

He exits the building and takes the long way to his apartment. As he walks through the crowd, he practices the right words to ask the housekeepers out for the evening.

After an hour's walk, he makes his way to the front entrance and greets the staff in the lobby before riding the elevator to his apartment.

He unlocks his door. As he steps inside, his mouth expands, his eyes widen, and his keys fall to the floor.

Standing before him were his two housekeepers, wearing sleeveless Cheongsam off-the-shoulder dresses. One had on a red color with long straight hair running down her back, and the other woman had on a black dress with her hair curled up with flowers.

He notices their curves, hugging their dress, and realizes they are twins with silky legs for days.

"You all are stunning. I would flood this entire apartment with money if I weren't maintaining abstinence. The night is young, so I might have to break my vows tonight."

"Thank you, Mr. Williams," they speak simultaneously.

The Chinese woman in the red dress points to his room. He looks in that direction, and the other woman informs him everything he needs is on the bed.

"Please shower and get dressed because the driver will be here in forty-five minutes," the woman in the black dress reveals.

"Why are Chinese people so impatience? Give me time to scrub my balls, and I'll be right back."

He marches to the master bedroom and showers. Devastation rises in the shower as his thoughts drift back to the women in the other room.

"Wait a minute. How did they know to be dressed when I came home?"

He ponders a minute longer. "That damn Diana. No wonder she mentioned I could ask my housekeepers."

He laughs, finishes his shower, and puts on the clothes lying on his bed.

He checks his time and completes the tasks in twenty minutes.

"Here I come!" he yells from inside the bedroom.

He appears in the kitchen within a few minutes, and they approve of the style they chose for him.

He escorts them downstairs, and the surprises keep coming. Outside is a luxury silver and black, all-electric SUV.

Devin pauses because he knows cars, and a Hongqi E-HS9 costs over $100,000.

The Chinese woman with the long hair reminds him, "are you going to stare at the car or get in? We have somewhere to go."

"Excuse me for being rude. Yes, I'm ready," he responds.

They sit in the back seat, and the driver closes the door and takes them to the club.

Devin hasn't explored Beijing since he arrived, and since he's in the mood to celebrate, he figures tonight would be a nice night to drink heavily.

He winks his eye at the ladies, stares out the window, and observes the nightlife culture along the way.

The driver announces, "Wǒmen zài zhèlǐ."

The drivers park the SUV and open the door for the ladies and Devin.

The line to get into the club was wrapped around the corner. "This is insane. We'll never get in here tonight," he mentions to the ladies.

DEVASTATION

They grab his hand and escort him to the front of the line and up the steps.

They got me following them like two housekeepers can break in front of the crowd, he thought.

The security guy detaches the chain from the pole and allows them to walk in without saying a word.

The ladies lead him upstairs to a private VIP booth overlooking the club.

"Drink whatever is on the table, and you can order more from the server. I'll be back with the owner soon," the long hair Chinese woman states and walks away.

He sits down, drinks, and converses with the other woman.

"Nice atmosphere. Do you all come here often?"

She didn't blink her eyes or part her lips while Devin was talking.

"Okay, I guess that's my cue to be quiet. Guess you're not happy to be here," he jokes.

The long hair Chinese woman returns with a black man who seems to belong to the silver fox beard club.

Devin was so excited to see another brother, he jumps up and spills his drink on one of the bodyguards.

"I'm sorry. Please excuse my clumsiness," he justifies.

The Chinese woman with the flowers in her hair shakes her head and laughs. She gives the mean-mugging guard a napkin to wipe his shirt.

The silver fox gentlemen lean over to the woman with the long hair. "Are you sure he's the one?"

"From what I was told, yes," she responds.

"Okay, let's get right to business. Mr. Williams, it's a pleasure to meet you. It's a shame you stop buying pussy because we have the best escorts in the country."

Devin mentions, "you sound like an associate I used to deal with back home."

The silver fox gentleman extends his hand to Devin. "Asperilla, I presume."

Devin shakes his head. "Wow, she got me again."

"No, she didn't send you this time. You can thank Malakai for this one."

Devin gasps and holds his chest; his hand trembles as he pours another drink. *He told me, a favor for a favor*, he remembers.

He clears his throat and shifts in his seat uncomfortably. Luckily for him, Ms. Yu Yan walks between the gentlemen and the straight-haired Chinese woman.

She kisses him on the lips and turns to Devin. "Welcome to the family. This is my husband, Kryptonite.

DEVASTATION

Standing alongside me is my daughter Mei and sitting beside you is Meiying. Be careful around her. She's only quiet because she's seen your tatted dick. She is waiting for you to get drunk, so she can cut it off and place it in her trophy case."

FLENARDO

DEVASTATION

Chapter 36

Devin unhooks the knot and pulls the tie from around his neck. He slings it on the couch as he walks through his apartment.

The meetup at the club seems more like an interrogation than a celebration. After hearing that Malakai endorsed him for a future job, his night of fun ends with a new family and a ton of stress.

"I need something to calm my nerves."

He walks to the wine cabinet and snatches a bottle of Sangria. He pops the cork and sniffs the aroma before turning it in the air and gulping it down his throat.

The wine runs out of the corner of his mouth and onto his clean white shirt.

He pulls the bottle from his lips and wipes his mouth with his sleeve.

He wonders if his promotion is a set up the whole time. The scariest part of the situation is the two assassins posing as maids. He heard urban legends about them, especially the one about them cutting a preacher's dick off during a happy ending massage.

He grabs Devastations through his pants. "Thank God we are practicing abstinence, but you deserve some attention."

He walks into the entertainment room, connects his smartphone to the TV, and searches through porn videos to relieve the stress from tonight.

This will be the first nut he will bust since his last sexual encounter with Armocita.

He places the wine bottle on the coffee table and slips out his pants and underwear. He looks around for some lotion, cream, or lubricant.

"I'm not about to walk into the bedroom to get that shit." He pours wine onto his hand, rubs his fingers together, and tugs on his dick.

He massages his dick and takes his free hand to find a video to erupt this much-needed milky volcano.

The first video that pulls up is titled *Becky and the Bus Ride*. The video's thumbnail shows a black man sitting with his back against a bus window and a white woman on her knees, sucking him off.

He raises his eyebrow and thinks, *what a weird caption,* but he's willing to watch anything to clear his mind.

He presses play, throws the phone down, and grabs his dick with two hands.

DEVASTATION

He elevates his pelvis in the air as his dick glides through the O-shape hole he creates with his hand.

He grabs some more wine, pours it over his hands, and grips his dick tighter as he watches the video. He wishes the woman in the video was sucking him off.

"Damn, this woman never comes up for air. The man is slaughtering her mouth, and she's swallowing that dick."

The guy on the bus snatches her hair and yanks the woman from his lap.

"What the fuck!" he yells.

His night couldn't get any worse. Right there, on his TV, is Veronica sucking this guy's dick.

He snatches the bottle and hurls it through the air. The bottle smashes into the TV and cracks the screen.

"Damn, this woman is stupid as shit! Everyone will know she's the biggest whore on the planet now."

He picks up the phone, unblocks her number, and taps her number fast and hard.

The phone rings in his ear. "I can't believe this woman."

He paces the room and waits for her to answer.

He looks down, and his dick is hard.

"Devastation, what the hell is wrong with you? You seriously can't be aroused from that sick shit."

The phone rings and goes to her voicemail.

"Veronica, call me back right now. I'm not playing with your ass."

He tosses the phone on the couch, runs to the kitchen, fills a pitcher with cold water, and emerges his dick.

He holds the pitcher between his legs and retrieves his phone.

"Hey Siri, call Ms. Shantae on speaker," he commands.

She answers on the third ring. "Good evening, Devin. Why aren't you sleeping? I know it's like 2 am over there," she answers.

"Well, I was going to have a solo moment with a video, but..." he confesses.

"Whoa! Too much info, Mr. Williams," she interrupts.

"I apologize, but did you know Veronica has become a porn star?"

"Devin, there are certain things I cannot discuss with you about my clients. Her last few sponsors aren't strong enough to handle her."

"Can't no one handle her ass," he admits.

"You can," Ms. Shantae responds. "She misses you, and you are her last lifeline."

"I just started my new job. I can't leave at this moment. It took me forever to get over here."

"Devin, I'll call you later. I have an appointment coming up, and there are more whores that need me. Let me know what time your flight lands," she mentions before hanging up the call.

It's moments like this he misses his locs. He has nothing to snatch, to keep him from going insane.

There's no pussy available for him to call. He has deleted all his apps, numbers, and websites.

"Ahhhhhhh!" he screams.

He takes the cold pitcher from between his thighs and pours the water down the drain.

He puffs his cheeks and blows the air out of his mouth. "You got this, Devin. Don't mess up your streak."

He closes his eyes and meditates. He inhales his tension and breathes it out. He repeats the cycle and feels his dick going limp.

He walks to his office desk, turns on his laptop, and searches the porn site. His first mission is to hack into the website and steal its credentials and money.

He sends a deadly virus so no one else can re-access it.

He pulls up another web page tab and searches for flights back to St. Louis. There's one that leaves before noon.

FLENARDO

He looks at the time on the computer screen, which reads 3 am. He's too angry to sleep, and every second counts when you are dealing with Vee.

He knows if too many people see the video, she might do something that will cause her to lose her life.

DEVASTATION

Chapter 37

Devin watches the wing flaps extend from his window seat as the airplane begins to descend. He imagines the cloud as a soft white pillow where he can rest his head in serenity.

The job in Beijing was an escape plan to leave his past behind, learn to love himself, and possibly find a woman to share his goals and dreams with.

The plane's wheel touches the runway and jolts a few more times before taxiing to the gate.

"Thanks for flying Air Canada. It was my pleasure to deliver you to the beautiful city of St. Louis," the pilot announces over the intercom.

Devin unbuckles his seat belt, stretches his legs, and retrieves his laptop bag from under the seat.

He stands and turns his head to the rear of the plane. *Thank God I always fly first class,* he thinks to himself.

He walks up the aisle, smiles at the Canadian flight stewardess, and follows the rest of the first-class passengers through the breezeway.

He speed walks through the terminal until he reaches the ground level. He slows down his stride, pulls out his phone, and contacts an Uber driver.

He smiles wide as Willie Wonka's profile appears as the driver nearby.

"Oh shit, I haven't seen this guy since I paid him to have fun with his wife. I can't wait for him to share the details."

He bypasses the panhandlers and dodges some ladies about to run into him as they rush from the drop-off lane to the airport.

He moves swiftly and stands under the Uber lane sign. The app informs him that Willie is two minutes away.

He switches screens and calls Vee. The phone rings until the annoying voicemail greeting says, "sorry, this mailbox is full. You are unable to leave a message at this time."

He grits his teeth and balls his fists. "Damn it, Vee. You know how to get under my skin. I flew halfway across the world to make sure you are ok."

A car horn beeps, and he looks up and sees Willie. His emotion shifts to excitement.

Willie rolls down the passenger window. "Get on in. I was waiting for you to order a ride one day."

DEVASTATION

Devin opens the door, sits in the passenger seat, and extends his arms toward Willie to accept a fist bump.

"Willie, my man! What's good? I know you have some good news to share with me."

"Devin, you have no idea how often I have wished your name would display on my screen."

"My apologies, Mr. Willie. I should have given you my phone number. I'll give it before I reach my destination."

"Great! But for now, you have to hear the fantastic news. We are expecting a baby," he discloses.

Devin begins to cough and laugh at the same time. "What the hell? Aren't you all a little elderly for kids?"

"This rocket still has some firepower left in the boosters," Willie jokes.

"Hey, I need to be like you when I become your age. Please don't leave me in the dark. I'm all ears for this story."

"As you suggested, I went home that night, and we role-played until the following day. Every weekend, we have created new characters and adventures since that night.

"One day, she went in for a checkup, and the doctor congratulated us on the new baby."

"Mr. Willie, you know you will be about seventy-seven at the high school graduation, right?"

"I believe God will provide for me to live healthy enough to enjoy that memory."

"I'm happy for you, Mr. Willie. Truly happy. If there's anything you ever need, never hesitate to ask."

"Thank you, Devin."

"Well, enough about me. Where are you coming from?" Mr. Wille asks.

"I'm living in Beijing now. I came home to check on a friend. I'm praying she's okay because she's going through an ugly situation."

"Devin, I have been living long enough to know that you will have some dreadful days and some lovely days. But, if you are breathing and above ground, you will learn to appreciate the ugliness in life and transform them into beautiful swans."

"Thanks for sharing that with me. I am accepting that in my life right now."

The car pulls into Vee's complex. Devin takes a deep breath. *I hope she's here*, he thinks.

"Mr. Willie, your tip is included. Oh, by the way, I'm texting you my phone number. Please text me your address, and I'll bring presents by for the baby shower early."

DEVASTATION

"Let us know the day you will be coming, and I'll have my famous St. Louis ribs waiting on you," Mr. Willie promises.

Devin grabs his computer bag, gives Mr. Willie another fist bump, and closes the door.

He waves and watches as Mr. Willie drives out of the parking lot and disappears down the street.

He slings his bag over his shoulder and marches around the building toward Vee's back patio.

He stops and wonders why Joe is tied up to a pole outside. "Poor Joe. Why are you out here looking all sad? Where's your Mama?" he asks while rubbing Joe's head.

He grips the handle on the storm door and pulls it, but it doesn't budge. He knocks on the glass pane. "Vee, it's Devin. Open the door!" he yells.

He looks down at Joe and notices his food and water is under the table.

Devin becomes concerned and irritated. He balls his fist tighter and bangs against the door. "Vee, open the fucking door!"

Fuck this shit. He wraps both hands around the handle, plants his feet, and jerks the door back and forth. The door releases from the hinges and pries open.

He runs into the house and finds Vee in her bedroom, crying with a gun barrel inside her mouth.

Shit, I'm not trained for this, he thinks.

She bites her teeth on the barrel and sputters, "Go away, Devin."

He drops his computer bag on the floor and inches closer to Vee. "I'm not going anywhere, and you're not, either.

"I'm still your sponsor, and we can get through this together. Please, Vee, can you remove the gun from your mouth?"

She slides the gun out of her mouth and presses it against her head. She laughs as the tears run down her face.

"Devin, don't come any closer, or I will squeeze the trigger. I'm never going to be anything but a whore. I'm sure you have seen the video. I didn't know it would be leaked across the internet.

"I'm better off dead. You, Ms. Shantae, Kaylene, and the whole class will become stress-free from my stupid decisions.

"I'm tired of my life. I'm tired of waiting for change to come. Death is the outcome for being an addict."

"Vee, please listen," he pleads. "I have been there—the constant desire and the itches that wake you out of your sleep. I'm afraid to pray because I fear all the sexual souls screaming inside me would drown out my cries for God.

"Veronica, look at me. Think of everything we have been through and survived."

She stares into his eyes and smiles. Within minutes her smile widens like a demonic entity. "I don't deserve you, Devin. I'm sorry."

Vee's index finger coils around the trigger as Devin runs towards her to save her.

"No, Veronica, no!" he screams.

She pulls the trigger and the gun jams. "Fuck my life. Not even the Devil wants a whore like me."

Devin slaps the gun from her hand, pulls her closer, and squeezes his arms around her back.

"You are still here, Vee. You are still here," he reminds her while rubbing her back.

She vomits on his shirt, and her arms and legs jerk uncontrollably.

"Vee, what did you do?"

He snatches out his phone and dials 911. He places the call on speaker as he tends to Vee.

"911, what is the address of your emergency?" the operator asks.

"My name is Devin Williams, and I believe my friend has taken some unknown drugs. Please send an ambulance to 4444 West Pine Boulevard, APT 108."

"Is the victim conscious or unconscious?" the operator asks.

"Conscious, but I'm not sure for how long," he responds.

"She is constantly throwing up, and her skin is sweaty and cold. Send someone quick. I can't lose her. I love her."

He holds her upright and attempts to keep her awake.

"Mr. Williams, the ambulance is on its way. Please monitor her breathing, and do you know how to perform CPR?"

"Yes, I do. I'll monitor everything until the ambulance arrives."

"Remain calm, and please stay on the phone until the ambulance arrives."

"I'll do whatever you ask. I'm not going anywhere.

"Don't give up, Vee," he whispers as he fights to keep her conscious.

DEVASTATION

Chapter 38

Vee hears a constant beeping sound; the more it beeps, the more aggravated she becomes.

Why doesn't someone cut that damn sound off?

She flickers her eyes lids and tries to make sense of the blurry images in front of her.

"Help," she cries softly.

She feels someone's fingers sliding into her hand. She yanks her hand away.

"Help," she cries again but a little louder than before.

"It's okay, Vee. It's me, Devin. You have been out for a while, but everything will be fine.

"Luckily, the EMS arrived to administer Naloxone and rushed you to the emergency room just in time."

She feels her left arm pulsating and turns her head to see what's happening.

"It's just an IV to help with dehydration," he mentions.

"What possessed you to swallow Percocets?"

She shrugs her shoulder, closes her eyes, and wishes Devin would stop asking questions.

"It's cool. You don't have to answer me, but I'm staying until you get help. I contacted Ms. Shantae while you were sedated."

She opens her eyes and blurts, "why did you do that? You are still meddling in my business, Devin. Take your ass back to Toyoko."

"Beijing," he corrects her before the doctor enters the room.

"You all sound like an old married couple," the doctor chimes in while walking over to Vee to check her vital signs.

"Ms. Hemsley, this isn't the first time you had a date with death," he mentions while shining the light in her eyes to check her pupils.

"Your chest X-rays are fine, no blood in your urine, but you're not leaving until we have someone to watch over you. If you decline to list a relative or friend, I have no choice but to call the police and have them sentence you to a live-in facility so you can be supervised 24/7.

"Those Percocets you were taking were illegal, and EMS found enough pill bottles under your bed to consider you a street pharmaceutical.

"I read through your medical records, and I'm sure you heard other doctors requesting rehabilitation for your drug abuse."

"Great, another class to sit in and tell people I'm a whore and druggie," she grumbles.

Devin steps towards the doctor. "If I can interject, please put my name on the paperwork."

The doctor turns to Vee for approval. She throws her hands up, frowns, and mumbles, "whatever."

"Okay, then. I'll have my nurse come in later and start the outpatient process. Ms. Hemsley, please be careful," he advises as he walks out of the room.

"I'm not sure why your ass is trippin', Vee. You know you want me around."

"You know I do, Daddy. Who else is going to keep me out of trouble?"

"Please don't call me Daddy. That shit sounds perverted, and you know we will never fuck."

"I just knew you were flying back to slay me with Devastation," she jokes.

"That's your fucking problem. You never take life seriously, but that shit is going to change. Starting today," he retorts.

"Okay, I'll do whatever you say but lower your tone. My head is throbbing like hell."

He walks to the recliner on the other side of the room, leans back, and attempts to take a power nap.

He is sexy when he's angry. I hope he knows I'm only going to therapy to be close to him, she ponders while looking at the heart rate monitor.

"Psst. Psst. Psst. Devin, I know you hear me."

He bounces from his position, kicking his legs and swinging his arms. "Vee, what the fuck do you want?"

"Nothinggggg," she hisses.

"Please leave me alone. I had a long flight and night, and it appears today will be even longer," he snaps.

He stands to his feet and stares at Vee. "Ok, you want my attention? You got it. Tell me why you took the pills."

"We're going there again?" she asks.

"Yes, and no bullshit this time."

She grabs the handrails and props herself up higher on the bed. "Okay, Devin, here's the truth.

"For the first time, I was embarrassed when you walked in on me having sex. I wish I could have handled the situation better. Explain how sorry I was or thank you for getting my rapist convicted.

"All you ever did was support me, but I felt abandoned when you left and stopped answering your phone. I started doing stupid shit, and the video was supposed to be for my eyes only. I had no idea everything would be leaked online."

He walks over, pulls some Kleenex from the box, and hands them to Vee.

"It's not all your fault. Maybe I should have done more as your sponsor.

"I hated the video, but my dick was hard as a rock. It's like the whore in me was turned on from seeing you treated like a slut bucket.

"Sorry for calling you a degrading name.

"I'm asking if you are willing to try a new path of cleansing our minds and bodies of this addiction. I'm not even sure we can call what we have an addiction. More like ASS-DICK-TIVE," he enunciates.

"That word is dope. Too bad the meaning is shitty," she jokes while wiping her tears and chuckling.

They share a laugh, and he walks over to hug her.

"It's okay, Vee. We are in this together," he reminds her and kisses her cheek.

He stares into her eyes and runs his finger over her hand. His heart beats faster, his lips tremble, and at this moment, he realizes the beauty Vee possesses.

He leans in slowly, and Vee anticipates a magical feeling she has long desired.

"Good news, Ms. Hemsley!" the nurse shouts while walking in and interrupting their moment.

He releases her hand, clears his throat, and stands beside the bed.

The nurse and her bad timing, she resonances through her mind while flashing a fake smile.

"Ms. Hemsley, I will remove your IV, help you get dressed, and sign off on your discharge paperwork."

"I'm going to step outside while you get dressed," Devin informs.

He stands outside the door. *Damn, I almost kissed Vee. It's too early for me. For us,* he thinks to himself.

He rocks back and forth against the wall while waiting for Vee to come out. As he remains in the hallway, he texts Ms. Yu Yan that he will return soon after he takes care of his personal affairs.

Vee bee-bops outside and yells, "I'm ready to go home, Daddy!"

DEVASTATION

He smiles, interlocks his arm inside hers, and leads her out of the hospital.

FLENARDO

DEVASTATION

Chapter 39

Vee drags her feet as she walks behind Devin, her heart is pounding inside her chest, and she feels like the hallway walls are closing in on her before she reaches Ms. Shantae's door.

She stops and leans against the wall. "Hold up, Devin. I'm not ready yet."

He turns around, places two fingers on her chin, and lifts her head.

His eyes connect with hers. "Vee, today is not a day of regrets or mistakes. Inside that room are people who love and care for you. Hell, I love you," he announces.

"Huh? What did you say?"

"That's a conversation for later. But for now, let's go ahead and conquer this obstacle together."

She wraps her hand around his wrist and follows him to the meeting.

She wishes she could skip the meeting and ask Devin why he loves her. She has always wanted to experience love but fears she will fuck it up and lose out with Devin.

She forces herself to smile and steps into the room behind Devin. The class cheers and claps as they walk in and take their seat.

Ms. Shantae smiles, runs over, and hugs Vee. "Never scare me like that again; I'm incredibly proud of you for coming today," she whispers.

"I'm sorry, Ms. Shantae. Please forgive me."

"You're alive, and that's what matters to me."

Ms. Shantae releases her hug, turns to Devin, and silently thanks him.

Ms. Shantae returns to the front of the class. "Thank you all for coming out tonight. It seemes like yesterday when Malakai decided to create sponsors for you all. I'm truly sorry he could not attend in person."

The room expresses their disappointment with boos and awes.

"Settle down, everyone. I'm sure you will see him again. For all I know, he's probably watching you from a hidden camera," she jokes.

"We do have a surprise for you all. Malakai's beautiful wife, Asperilla, is on Microsoft Teams. She will present the money to the most devoted sponsor team."

Ms. Shantae turned on the projectors and logged into her laptop.

DEVASTATION

"Almost there, class," she mentions while making sure the connection goes through.

"Asperilla, can you see and hear us?" Ms. Shantae asks.

"Yes, loud and clear. Wow, new technology!

"Congratulations, you all have achieved your Cum-laude diplomas. The highest achievement after that is a Bukkake diploma. To graduate from that, you have to form a circle, similar to what you are in now, and a group of guys will go from person to person ejaculating success over you.

"Ejaculate to Congratulate! Oh shit, that's funny as hell!" She laughs as the class throws their hands up and wonders what the hell is happening.

"Damn, I guess that wasn't funny to a bunch of serious-minded muthafuckers," she speculates.

"Okay, Malakai promised someone a million dollars. That sounds great, but you are only receiving five hundred thousand. I know where everyone lives and if we have a problem, I promise you won't see tomorrow," she threatens them by sliding a knife across her neck.

The room became silent, and no one blinked or moved a muscle.

"Umm, it appears I'm still crazy as ever. Relax, I'm only fucking with you all," she states and begins to shuffle some papers.

"The most extended team that went without fucking is Sarah and Bruno. Sarah and Bruno, please raise your hand, or the money will stay with me," she proclaims.

The team raises their hands, and the rest of the group cheers and claps for them.

Bruno and Sarah's phones chirp from an incoming text. Their hands tremble as they read the message and watch Asperilla on the screen.

"In good faith, we have decided not to take Malakai's initial amount. We will take half and reward the rest of the teams with $25,000 each for completing this journey with us," Bruno offers.

Bruno stares at the screen and watches Asperilla smile and clap her hands.

Ms. Shantae claps her hands and says, "let's congratulate Bruno and Sarah one more time. Enjoy your money, spend it, but remember your promise to live better."

"If you fuck up, I will be there to collect interests, and being in debt to me will make your former lifestyle seem like child's play. I wish you the best in your new life," Asperilla salutes and disconnects from the video.

DEVASTATION

Sarah raises her hand. "Ms. Shantae, what does she mean by interest?"

"All I can say is do right with your money, find a committed relationship, and don't return to your old life," Ms. Shantae informs her before disconnecting her laptop.

Vee looks over at Devin and asks, "why are you involved with merciless individuals?"

"Vee, you don't want to know the answer. Let's just say every favor comes with a price. Saving you was worth it, and I'll sacrifice myself all over again for you," he admits.

He stands up, looks around the room, and drops to one knee. He pulls out a 1.5 carat diamond skull ring from his pocket.

Vee gasps and places her hands over her mouth.

The class stops chattering, and everyone's eyes shift to Devin's next move.

"Veronica Marie Hemsley, I hated you from the moment we met, but I also know my life wouldn't be shit unless you were in it. I have done some of the stupidest things on Earth."

She drops her hands from her mouth. "I have, too," she interrupts.

"Vee, stop talking before you make me forget what I need to say."

She taps her feet on the floor and throws her hands back over her mouth.

"Vee, we belong together, and I'm giving my heart to you if you are willing to nurture it into something incredible. I know we aren't the perfect couple; we are two whores in rehab, striving to find happiness. I'm tired of adding bodies to my soul. I need to know if you are tired too and if not, I will wait but don't accept this ring unless you are sure."

He lifts the ring higher in the air, drops his head, and prays she responds correctly.

"I think…"

He lifts his head. "No, Veronica. I need to know if you are tired."

She looks around the room and sees Ms. Shantae grinning from ear to ear.

She stares at the beautiful ring and shouts, "yes! I'm tired of my life and I'm willing to change for us."

She extends her hand, and Devin slides the ring on her finger. She reminisces on the moment they were in the hospital and were moments away from sharing a kiss.

Devin whispers, "I got you, Vee."

He leans in and kisses her soft wet glossy lips. The cool peppermint lip balm melts on his tongue.

DEVASTATION

He breaks away from the kiss, stands to his feet, and lifts Vee from her seat.

Everyone claps and cheers for the magical encounter between two of the most opposite people in the group.

Vee leans in on his shoulder. "Where do we go from here?" she ask.

"I have no idea, but every day will be spontaneous. We will create more extraordinary memories outside the bedroom."

"What the fuck! You proposed to me, and I can't feel Devastation?"

He laughs and kisses her cheek. "In time, Vee, in time. But for now, let's get the fuck out of here."

They shake hands and hug their fellow members as they walk through the circle and out the door.

FLENARDO

Chapter 40

Vee positions herself between Devin's legs as the sky metamorphoses into shades of red, orange, and pink. The evening is approaching, and they will wait until the stars align before they leave the park.

She squeezes her right eye closed and lifts her hand in the air, wondering if her engagement ring will twinkle like the stars.

"I see you are fascinated by your engagement ring. It looks perfect on you," Devin recalls.

"I can't believe you asked me to marry you. I'm still in shock over the proposal. I'm even more shocked that we have been on numerous dates and still haven't slept together.

"I can't tell you the last time I cuddled in bed with a man and didn't have sex."

"It's strange, but we can't rush sexual feelings over healing. We have to do things right this time," he insists.

He braids a strand of her hair and kisses her left earlobe. "Don't worry. We are going to explore climax without penetration," he whispers.

"Oh really? I'll believe it when I see it," she responds before releasing an orgasmic sigh.

"Who taught you how to braid hair?"

"I used to loc my hair, but those days are long gone. I would rather play in yours."

She scrolls through her iPad, finds a novel to read, and relaxes while Devin works his fingers through her hair.

Devin inhales the perfume seeping from her neck, and Vee jumps as Devastation thumps under her butt.

"Devin, you better stop fucking with me unless you are going to fuck me," she purrs.

"Duly noted," he responds.

He braids her hair into two pigtails. "I love this look on you. Such a turn-on," he compliments.

She leans back, and they exchange glances and smile at each other.

"Devin, I love you," she acknowledges.

"I love you too."

His phone rings a distinctive ringtone, and he already knows who's on the other end.

DEVASTATION

"Hold that memory, and I'll add more when I return," he promises.

He slides her over, picks himself up from the ground, and walks toward the lake.

"Shí jiān dào le," Ms. Diana mentions to him.

"Yes, I know my time is up. My plane will depart Sunday. I haven't found the right time to tell Vee yet."

"There's no time like the present," she suggests and hangs up the phone.

"Shit! They don't play about their money.

"Okay, Devin, just let her know you have to leave for a few weeks. No, that will never work."

He stares at the sky; if ideas could fall from above, it would surely knock him on the head.

He turns around and yells Vee's name while sprinting back to her. His voice startles Joe, and he jumps up to meet Devin.

"Vee, I need you to hear me out. And whatever you do, don't tell me no."

"Calm down, Devin. I'm listening," she answers while putting away her iPad.

"How would you like to come to Beijing with me?"

What the fuck am I supposed to do over there? she questions herself.

"Before you say anything, I thought it all out. We can fly Kaylene over there as many times as you like. We can continue our video calls with Ms. Shantae. The best part is there won't be any temptations around you. I'm about the only piece of chocolate your ass will ever see," he jokes.

"Okay. You are planning to take me to a distant land where my tatted gothic ass will stand out like a sore thumb."

"Precisely," he replies.

"Okay, sounds cool. I'll eat edibles and learn a new language while I'm there. When do we leave?" she asks.

"Sunday."

"Devin, that's two days away! I can't get everything packed in time," she says.

"We'll come back and get whatever you need. Right now, it's all about you, me, and Joe."

She laughs and shakes her head. "Wow, this evening is getting crazier. Are you ready to leave so I can start packing?" she asks.

"Not quite," he states while making Joe lie down.

He stoops down to her level and flashes his sexy dimples that she enjoys forming on his face.

"You deserve to be kissed," he mentions while placing her hands on his chest.

DEVASTATION

"Lie down," he commands.

She leans across the blanket and closes her eyes.

She feels his hands trailing down her legs and without warning, those hands creep between her thighs.

Her legs shake, and she bites her lip. *Oh shit, I have waited forever for this moment. I'm glad I wore a dress,* she thinks to herself.

He drops to his knees, crawls backward on the blanket, and slides his head under her dress.

"Your smell is breathtaking, and I want you to take my breath away when I taste you," he informs.

"Mmm," she moans and shakes her head while swirling her finger over her nipples.

He swipes his tongue on her inner right thigh, switches left, and blows his warm breath over her clit.

He opens her lips, stirs his finger inside, and alternates between his tongue and finger.

She opens her eyes and watches her dress rise and fall from Devin pouncing his head between her thighs.

Vee moans softly and throws her legs in the air while Devin slurps his tongue around her honeypot.

She rubs her hands over his head as he suctions his mouth and pulls her lips while retracting his head backward.

FLENARDO

"Oh my God!" she cries.

He intensifies his licks, grips his nails into her ass cheeks, and plunges his tongue inside her walls.

"Ooh. Ohh," she moans and reaches for his dick, but he slaps her hand away.

"No baby, this pleasure is for you. Just feed me," he demands.

He turns her over, and she props up on her knees.

He eats her from behind, and she jiggles her asscheeks before slamming into his face.

"I love you, Vee," he mutters while tasting her.

"If you love me, then fuck me!" she screams.

"Not yet. You aren't ready for that."

He slides away, releases his drawstring, and slides his pants down to his ankles. "Ride my face, and I'll beat Devastation for you."

"I've always wanted to see you cum," she says while mounting him.

He wraps his arms around her thighs. She looks over her shoulder and sees his thick, tatted dick dripping precum.

Stay the course, Vee. Don't suck it, she reminds herself while recoiling on his face.

She distracts herself by turning her head and swishing her fingers across her pussy lips while riding his face harder.

She yanks her dress over her head and returns to riding Devin's face. "Ooh, I've been nice long enough. Eat this pussy. Suck my juices. Make me cum. Show me how much you love me!" she screams.

Her words stimulate his soul. He squeezes two hands around Devastation, slamming his fists down, and yanks them back up. He arches his hips and continues to eat her while jacking his dick.

"Vee," he groans.

"Yes, Devin?" she moans.

"I shoot a lot," he informs her while breathing and stroking his dick.

"Me too, Daddy, don't stop," she begs.

Tears form in her eyes. She has never experienced pleasure from a man of this magnitude. Deep down, she knows she cannot fuck this up.

She thrusts her hips and bucks on his face. Devin's tongue matches her pace.

"Cum with me, Devin. Please cum with me!" she hollers.

"Oh, shit, Vee. I'll cum for you."

She flickers her fingers faster, and he strokes more quickly, and neither care who cums first.

Vee rides his face, flapping her clit, and moaning louder. She feels Devin's hips fall to the ground, and without notice, a hot rush of cum splatters her ass cheeks and goes up her back.

He lifts her a few inches away from his face and smiles. "Cum for me, Veronica Marie," he whispers.

She watches his lips roll out her name, and she spreads her pussy wider and squirts the hardest she ever has in her life.

The stream floods Devin's face and runs onto the blanket. She throws her head back and falls upon his chest.

"Whew! I wasn't expecting all of that today. Do you need some wipes, a towel, or another face?" she asks.

"I'm good. Just lie here for a moment," he suggests, wrapping his arms around her back.

"Devin, do you think we will regret this?" she asks.

"We are two whores in rehab. We're going to mess up, but this time, all the mess will be on us and in us," he explains.

"I love the sound of that," she responds.

"Me too, baby. Me too."

If you love DEVASTATION, then prepare yourself for a small taste of my next novel, "Relationship Killer."

Dominic sits quietly in the woods, observing his wife having sex with another man in their bed.

He noticed her behavior was off from the moment she dropped him off on base to catch the bird to Afghanistan nine months ago.

He watches Tyrese, his best friend of seven years, the guy he fought wars with and helped deliver his first-born son, dive his face between his wife Jennifer's legs.

Dominic wonders how Tyrese's wife, Mary, will feel when she finds out Tyrese is fucking his wife.

"Jennifer, I'm not going to cry over you, but the world will know you were the one that awakened the beast inside of me. I gave you everything, and this is how you are going to repay me? I'm going to make sure everyone feels my pain," he talks to himself while putting away the binoculars.

Since his time in Afghanistan, he has made friends with influential leaders. One IED and a bogus flight to Ramstein was all it took for him to be sitting a mile and a half behind his house in the dark woods.

He sings an Army cadence to motivate himself to take another life.

Your baby was lonely, as lonely could be /
Til Tyrese provided the company
Ain't it great to have a pal /
Who works so hard just to keep up morale?
Sound off! / 1,2
Sound off! / 3,4
Cadence count now! / 1,2,3,4,1,2...3,4!

He picks up his sniper rifle and looks into the scope. His wife has climbed on top Tyrese, and he is gripping her asscheeks as she rides his dick.

He has calculated the dimensions and distance to fire a bullet from his location and hit his target.

He places his cheek against the butt stock, gently caresses the trigger, and breathes slowly as he waits for the perfect shot.

Tyrese, you haven't changed one bit since we met. You still love fucking women with the lights on. Perfect for me. Deadly for you, he thinks to himself as he squeezes the trigger.

He remains calm as the bullet sails through the air. At this moment, time slows down as he reminisces on the good times with Jennifer and how much he loved her to death.

All that changed as the bullet pierced the bedroom window and struck her in the head at the precise time she stood on her toes, as she continued to ride Tyrese's dick.

Dominic originally planned to kill Jennifer, frame Tyrese, and watch him suffer in jail. It was a vicious idea, but Mary and the kids deserve his Servicemember Life Insurance.

Inside the crossbeam, Dominic watches Tyrese push Jennifer's lifeless body off him and attempt to seek cover.

Muthafucker didn't even care for his wife. All she was to him was another side chick.

Fuck you, Tyrese, he thinks to himself, as he squeezes the trigger.

The bullet enters the side of his forehead and knocks him to the floor while he runs toward the master closet.

Dominic climbs down from his tree stand, packs away his rifle, and quickly tears down his sniper post.

Before sunrise tomorrow, he will be on his way back to Germany, and with the help of some influential leaders, no one will ever know he came home.

Flenardo Speaks

Flenardo is an ordinary man who foreplays his dreams into reality with creative strokes of imaginative superpowers. His passion for doing the unthinkable is his adrenaline rush toward the next adventure.

Thank you for reading DEVASTATION. You are welcome to post amazon reviews and share your social media love with your friends.

I love chatting with all my supporters. You can connect with me by joining my newsletter for upcoming novels, tours, intimate book discussions, & book signings

Made in the USA
Columbia, SC
12 November 2024